A KNIGHT
TO REMEMBER

by

HERMIONE MOON

DEDICATION

To Tony & Chris, my Kiwi boys.

CONTENTS

Catch Up

A Knight to Remember is the third book in The Avalon Café series of cozy witch mysteries that feature me, Gwen Young, and my adventures in the town of Glastonbury, England. Each book features a standalone murder mystery, but my personal story continues through the series. Because of this, if you haven't read it already, you might like to start with *One Dark and Stormy Knight* (Book 1). But here's a short summary of the story so far if you're beginning here or just need to refresh your memory.

All the women in my family are witches. Most of us do spells through our baking, using herbs and ingredients we bless to help people, and I sell my products in The Avalon Café, which is opposite the beautiful Glastonbury Abbey in Somerset, England.

My dad died when I was four, and my mother died not long ago from complications due to Multiple Sclerosis. I'm now twenty-nine. I left university to look after Mum, and I hadn't dated anyone since my first boyfriend, Luke, so I've been a little lonely, especially since Mum died.

And then I met Arthur.

Yes, King Arthur—except he insists he wasn't a king. He was a warrior in the sixth century, after the Romans left Britannia, and he led an army that stopped the Saxons invading for many years before he was mortally wounded at the Battle of Camlann.

But he didn't die. His sister, Morgana, also a witch, transferred his soul to a soulstone, a ruby, which ended up in the pommel of a sword, part of a suit of armour that stood in my café as long as I can remember. And then Arthur woke up.

He insists I'm the reincarnation of his wife, Guinevere, and my dog Merlin is his old friend, the bard Taliesin. I had the ruby set in a gold ring, and Arthur was able to take off the suit of armour.

Since then, we've solved two murder mysteries, and have discovered that the people involved were members of a coven of witches called Morgana's Sisters. And here we are, at the beginning of May, about to start another case.

Oh, one more thing—Arthur and I are dating. He's very old-fashioned and wants to win my heart all over again, and I'm happy to let him!

Chapter One

I'm standing on a cliff edge, looking down at the sea.

It's a bright, blustery day. The wind tugs at my clothes and whips my hair around my face. Seagulls dip and soar before me, riding the currents. Several hundred feet below, the white-tipped waves claw at the rocks.

I'm with a man. He's medium height, with cropped light-brown hair and a neatly trimmed beard. He's wearing a navy-blue business suit with a white shirt and a light-blue tie, and he looks somehow incongruous in this wild setting.

He bends his head and kisses me, taking his time, his lips moving across mine tenderly. I rest my hands on his chest, holding his lapels. We turn slowly in the blustery wind, and the sun is hot on my face. I'm filled with love for him. I'm crazy about this guy. I've been in chains for so long, but the two of us are nearly free. Now that we've placed all the stones, I think he's going to ask me to marry him. It is Beltane, after all, a time of courtship rituals and lovemaking. I'm so happy. I lift my arms around his neck, and, behind his head, I pull off my old wedding ring and drop it to the ground. I feel free as a bird.

He lifts his head and looks into my eyes. I expect to see the love, the adoration he's shown me over the past few weeks.

Instead, to my shock, his blue eyes are cold, and he's not smiling.

My heart misses a beat. It takes only a second—a fraction of a second—for me to realize what he's about to do. A heartbeat later, he places his hands on my shoulders and pushes me hard.

I stumble on the uneven rock. Then there's no more ground, and I tumble backward.

My scream is lost amongst the crash of the waves.

I turn in the air, arms flailing, and now I'm facing down, looking at the rapid approach of the cruel grey rocks.

I thought he loved me. But he was just using me to get what he wanted.

I think of Arthur and the part I've played in his downfall. I'm surprised to feel a stab of regret. But it's too late for me to do anything about it.

The seagulls cry, but nobody will cry for me.

*

"Gwen?"

I blink furiously at Arthur's voice, putting out my hands to steady myself as the sensation of falling makes me feel as if I'm going to tip over. I'm sitting, though, on the sofa in my quiet living room. The fire is crackling away in the hearth, as it's still cool in the evenings, even though it's the first of May today. Most nights, Merlin stretches out by it, but at the moment he's sitting in front of me, his Labradoodle face managing to look concerned.

Arthur puts the book on astronomy that he was reading onto the coffee table and moves closer to me, taking my hand in his. "Are you okay?" he asks. "You're so pale, your freckles have almost disappeared." Gently, he removes the Tarot card I was holding and studies it. It's the Queen of Cups. "What happened? Did you have a vision?"

I nod. "I didn't think it would work," I whisper. "I've been studying for weeks, and I haven't had a single image pop into my head. And then this happens... It was so vivid, so real." I swallow hard at the thought of the rocks approaching at an alarming speed.

"Wait here," Arthur says, rising. "I'm going to get you a whisky."

I don't argue with him. I could do with a stiff drink.

He goes out of the room, and I open my arms as Merlin comes up to me. He jumps onto the sofa, sits beside me, and licks my hand. I put my arm around him, comforted and grounded by his warmth. Most of the time, I try to think of him as Taliesin, the bard and poet, and Arthur's friend, but at times like this the dog part of him is even more important to me.

"Did you see her, too?" I whisper. Merlin is psychic, sent here to help lost souls find their way to the Summerlands, as he calls Heaven.

Merlin sneezes as Arthur comes back in carrying two tumblers filled with ice and the red-gold liquid that must be Glenfiddich. He sits on the other side of Merlin and hands me one glass, and I take a big mouthful and swallow. I cough but welcome the sear of it down my throat.

Arthur takes a sip out of his glass, looking at Merlin. "He says he felt a presence, but he didn't have a vision. He says he can only see mist. He's a bit confused." Arthur lifts his blue-eyed gaze to me. "What did you see?"

I have another mouthful of whisky to boost my courage. "I was standing on a cliff top, looking over the sea. I was with a man in a suit, and he kissed me. I was so happy… I thought he was going to propose. And then he pushed me over the cliff." I shiver at the memory. "I was just about to hit the rocks when you called my name."

"You cried out," he says. "Did you know the woman?"

"I don't know. I was looking through her eyes—maybe it was me." The thought chills me. "Perhaps it was a vision of the future."

"I'm assuming the man wasn't me?" Arthur says.

"No, no, he was shorter than you, with light-brown hair and a beard." Arthur has dark hair and is clean-shaven most of the time, although I know he had a beard back when he was alive in the sixth century.

"Then it wasn't you in the vision," he states firmly. "I'm the only one who's going to be kissing you anytime soon."

I suppose I should complain at his possessive tone, but as I look up into his eyes, I'm warmed through.

"All right," I murmur. He clicks his fingers to get Merlin to lie down, then puts his arm around my shoulder and pulls me close for a kiss.

I try not to think about how the man kissed me on the cliff top and concentrate instead on the feel of Arthur's lips pressed against mine. Like an artist, he has a colourful palette of kisses to choose from. I discovered this because we've been kissing a lot over the five weeks since we solved the murder of who killed Valerie Hopkins-Brown.

Sometimes he's playful, placing butterfly kisses across my mouth and cheeks and nose. At other times he turns up the dial, going from sexy teasing to full-on hot-as-the-sun smooches that make me tingle all over.

But today he's gentle, pressing his lips to mine two, three, four times, then, as Merlin jumps down, Arthur pulls me into his arms and holds me tightly.

"Did you recognize the man?" he asks, rubbing my back.

"No."

"The place?"

"No. It was just a cliff. I suppose it could have been Dorset." I curl up against him, enjoying the feel of his muscular body against mine as I sip my whisky.

He puts down his glass and picks up the Tarot card again. "So was it the card that triggered the vision?"

"I think so." We both study the figure of the Queen of Cups. She's beautiful, dressed in a green gown, sitting inside a large shell by the sea. "I was shuffling through the cards," I explain, "and I turned over this one, so I tried to relax and meditate on it, letting my gaze focus on the images while I cleared my mind. I've done this dozens of times, but it's the first time I've seen anything."

Every witch has her favourite form of divination—a method of seeking knowledge of the future or the unknown. Mum used her crystal ball, my grandmother, Lizzie, loved her runes, my great-great-grandmother read tea leaves, and her mother could tell a person's future by examining the lines on their palm.

I've never been great at it, though, and I was content to work my magic through my baking, casting mild spells with herbs and spices. But since I saw an image in Mum's crystal ball five weeks ago, I've been working on my divination skills.

In the first week, I studied the crystal ball, hoping I would see images in it again. But all I saw was the reflection of my own eyes, upside down in the glass.

It was Arthur's suggestion that I try using Tarot cards. He told me his sister, Morgana, used a form of cartomancy to aid her psychic talents, and this prompted me to give the Tarot a go.

I bought the deck I'm using a few years ago and tried to use it a few times, but nothing much happened, and I figured I had no skill in that area. But it seems my witchy talents are growing.

"The cards are beautiful." Arthur turns the Queen of Cups over in his fingers.

"It's called The Robin Wood Tarot." I pick up the box containing the other cards and show him the picture on the front. "I was drawn to it because of this image. It's the Magician, which is the second card in the deck."

"It's got a number one on it."

"Yes, but the Fool is the first card—his number is zero." I rub my thumb across the Magician. He's a handsome man, dressed in red robes, wearing a stag's head and antlers. He's balancing a glowing infinity symbol on his right hand. "He reminds me of you," I say distractedly.

"In what way?"

"He's a part of English myth. His picture convinced me to buy the deck."

I can still remember the moment I saw the pack in the bookshop. I don't know how long I stood there, staring at the picture, but I feel the same intense connection now that I felt then as I study him and the tools of his trade on the table—the cup, sword, pentacle, and wand. He personifies England, and he carries within him the masculine magic that's woven through history. He's a druid, the consort of the Goddess and the heart of England. I can trace him back through time, to the legends of Robin Hood and King Arthur. And even further back, to the pagan earth gods, Herne the Hunter and the Green Man, men of the field and the forest, who supply their seed to allow the Mother to bring forth life…

"Gwen!"

I snap to and blink at Arthur. He's frowning at me. Gods, he's so handsome.

"Sorry," I say. "I think it's something to do with Beltane. I feel all…" My voice trails off. I don't know what I'm saying, and I blush.

"Beltane, eh?" Arthur murmurs, and he slides a knuckle under my chin and lifts it so I'm looking into his eyes.

I hold my breath. We've been living together for six weeks now. We've kissed every day for the last five, usually more than once. When he first came out of the suit of armour, I told him that I needed time before our relationship turned physical. He replied that he was happy to wait until I was ready. And so, even though we've been kissing, he's been the perfect gentleman.

Only I could be in love with a man with principles.

I've tried to pluck up the courage several times over the past few days to talk to him about it. But the truth is that I don't know where to start. My mother was a very private person, and even though she was loving, we didn't talk much about feelings. My one relationship was years ago. I haven't slept around. I'm naturally shy and reserved. So I have no idea how to tell Arthur that he's waited long enough.

I open my mouth to speak, but Arthur just smiles, leans forward, and kisses my forehead before turning away to pick up his drink, and the moment's gone. His gaze is distant as he sips his whisky, and for a moment he feels a long way away from me.

With sudden clarity, I remember the last thoughts of the woman as she tumbled from the cliffs.

He was just using me to get what he wanted... I think of Arthur and the part I've played in his downfall. I'm surprised to feel a stab of regret. But it's too late for me to do anything about it.

I'd forgotten that. The woman in my vision is somehow connected to Arthur.

Cold slithers down through my body. Who was she? And how does she know him?

Chapter Two

It's now the fourth of May, and the rain of the past few weeks has given way to bright sunshine and warm afternoons.

I'm working with my assistant, Delia, in the kitchen around one p.m. on Monday afternoon when my mobile rings in my jeans pocket. I take it out, thinking it might be my friend Imogen wanting to organize a double date again, but the screen reads Beatrix, and I answer it with a smile.

"Hey you!" I nod at Delia to continue making what I call my Magic Muffins—a healthy recipe of bran and banana with double-blessed cinnamon and other spices that's guaranteed to give a lift to even the lowest of spirits—and walk over to look through the kitchen window of the café while I chat. It's busy today, but Delia's sister, Melissa, is organized and unflappable, and she keeps Cooper, the barista, and Tamara, the new young waitress he has his eye on, in check and working hard.

"Hello, sweetheart," my aunt replies. "How are you doing?"

"I'm good, thank you. What are you up to? Busy painting?" Beatrix is also a witch, but she does her magic through her artwork, using ingredients in her paint and imbuing the pictures with positive energies.

"I will be, this afternoon," she replies. "I had my art class this morning."

"Oh yes, of course, it's Monday."

Beatrix is a big believer in the healing power of art and creativity, and she enjoys sharing her talent with others. As well as running two adult education art classes, she also visits retirement homes and encourages the elderly to take part in fun painting exercises.

"Mm," she continues. "A funny thing happened today."

"Oh?" I watch as Cooper murmurs something to Tamara that makes her laugh, and I smile. I believe they're going to a party together on Friday night. I think they'll be good together.

"One of my students didn't turn up for class," Beatrix says. "Charlotte Small is her name. That in itself isn't startling—of course people are sometimes sick or have other commitments. But I was talking to one of the other students who knows her, and she said apparently Charlotte hasn't been seen since Friday."

I continue staring through the window, but I'm not seeing the scene before me. My mind is whirling, and I feel a little nauseous.

Charlotte went missing on the same day as the woman in my vision who fell off the cliff.

A coincidence, surely?

"She's married," Beatrix carries on, oblivious to my fears, "although apparently her husband is a bit of a slob. I don't think he's reported her missing yet. The other student says she gave them both a lift once when their car broke down, and there's no love lost between them. She said they argued all the way to town. But anyway, that's not the strangest thing."

"What else?" I ask faintly.

"I've had my students working on a project for the past few weeks, trying to encourage them to use their imagination and not always feel as if they have to make everything realistic. Charlotte is a skilled artist, and she threw herself into the project with gusto. She's been painting a picture of a stylized Glastonbury Tor. It's very good. It's also... weird."

It's an odd word for Beatrix to use, who doesn't normally criticize people like that. "In what way?" I query.

"Well, I realized after her first few lessons that she's obsessed with the legend of King Arthur. Every drawing or painting she does features him in some way. And that's fine—it's a free country, and we do live in Glastonbury, after all. But this painting... well... I'd like to show it to you. Can I bring it over later?"

"Of course." I remember something that Arthur suggested a few days ago. "We were wondering whether you and Max would like to come for dinner at some point. Why don't we make it tonight?"

"Oh, are you sure?"

"Definitely. You know how well Arthur gets on with Max. It should be fun."

"All right then. What time?"

"Seven?"

"I'll see you then." She pauses. "Gwen… are you okay? I haven't upset you?"

"No, not at all. Something's on my mind, that's all. I'll tell you about it tonight."

"Okay. See you later." She hangs up.

I slide my phone back into my pocket, but don't yet return to Delia. Outside, the sky has clouded over, and a shiver of unease runs down my spine.

I'm still looking through the window facing the café, but I'm lost in thought. My vision blurs, and my gaze shifts to the reflection in the window. I can see Joss, my assistant, stacking the dishwasher, and Delia placing the trays of muffins in the oven.

And next to them, as clear as if she's standing behind me, is the figure of a shortish blonde woman, maybe mid-thirties, a little overweight and frumpy, dressed in grey trousers and an unflattering blue sweater. She's watching me, and there are tears on her cheeks.

I whip around, but nobody's there.

I look at the doorway to the kitchen. Merlin is sitting there, watching me. He's been in the break room for the past hour, snoozing, but I can tell he's seen the figure.

Feeling shaky, I tell Delia I'm done for the day, collect my handbag and jacket, say goodbye to the others, go out with Merlin past Sir Boss—the suit of armour that stands in the doorway—and head into the blustery afternoon.

I finish work at the café around two p.m. most days now. Kit Vinson, the new head of the unit who started a few weeks ago, turned out to be a hardworking and open-minded guy who was more than happy to allow me to help out, cleaning and cataloguing artefacts, doing research, and occasionally going out with him, Duncan, and Una to take part in a dig. We got on so well that he offered me a paid, part-time role as an assistant archaeologist, and I work there on Mondays and Fridays, from two until five.

I think if I had a degree, he'd take me on full time, but I had to leave university to look after my mum when she was too sick to work. Arthur's been trying to talk me into finishing my degree part-time. So far, I've used the excuse that I don't want to give up working at the café, which is true, as I love my job. But I've been too embarrassed to admit that I can't afford to pay for the course, and I don't want to take out a loan. The money my mother left me has dwindled away, and I don't want to spend the small amount left, as it's nice to have a cushion in case the car needs fixing or something in the house needs replacing.

Over a month ago, Arthur led me to an urn filled with old Roman coins that he buried back in the sixth century, because he wanted to be able to contribute financially. I helped Duncan and Una to excavate it, and they've sent it to the coroner's office to be valued, but I know it takes a while for the money to come through, and anyway, I have no idea how much it's going to be. There were some silver coins in there, but that doesn't mean it's worth a fortune.

And even if it is, I'm not sure I should take it from him. We're not married now, and he doesn't owe me anything.

I sigh, heading with Merlin across to the field unit. I don't know why I'm feeling maudlin today. It's not like me at all. I push my melancholy away and paint a smile on my face as I go into the field unit, determined to enjoy myself for the next couple of hours. Then I can go home and spend some time cooking something nice for dinner.

*

"I'll get it," Arthur says as the doorbell rings, and he goes out of the kitchen to answer the door. I check once more on the herb spring chicken pot pie and roasted vegetables in the oven, then turn with a smile as he returns with Beatrix and Max, laughing as they fuss Merlin, who's jumping up and down at the sight of them.

"Hey, you two." I give them both a kiss on the cheek. Beatrix looks lovely this evening. Usually she wears jeans or slacks and T-shirts, as most of the time she has her painting apron over her clothes, but tonight she's wearing a pretty knee-length dress covered in green and pink flowers, and she's pinned up the side of her silver hair with a pink rose clip. "You look gorgeous," I tell her.

"You too," she replies, smiling. "You have such a amazing pair of legs! You should show them more. Shouldn't she, Arthur?"

"Absolutely." He winks at me. I laugh and turn back to the worktop, where I'm finishing off the starter of smoked salmon with prawns, horseradish cream, and lime vinaigrette, full of lovely spring flavours. I've blessed the tarragon and parsley in the chicken pot pie with a general happiness spell to make the evening go well, not that I have to worry about that really, as Beatrix and Max are the easiest people in the world to get along with, and I know they love Arthur too.

Unusually for me, tonight I've opted for a black skirt that comes to above my knees with black opaque tights and a tight blue sweater—nothing like my usual floor-length boho skirts and loose blouses. Secretly, I want Arthur to notice my figure. I'm hoping it might help speed things along a little in our relationship.

I put the finishing touches to the starters, then join the others at the pine kitchen table. Beatrix is still standing, holding a piece of board, its back to us. I've already briefed Arthur on what she told me earlier, so he knows this is the piece of art that the missing Charlotte has been working on.

As I sit, Beatrix turns the board around.

It's clearly a painting of Glastonbury Tor. I recognize the shape, and on top of it St. Michael's Tower, the last remaining piece of the church that once stood there.

But that's where the reality ends. The mound is surrounded by swirls of colour painted in stripes. Blues, oranges, and reds fill the sky, possibly denoting a sunrise or a sunset. The bottom contains more blues, greens, and browns, which I'm sure is supposed to reflect that this area was once a land of swamps and lakes, traversed by wooden walkways.

It's oddly beautiful and haunting, but there are more interesting things about it than the psychedelic colours.

For a start, Charlotte has written the name Arthur in tiny script hundreds and hundreds of times along each stripe of colour.

"Wow." I bend to examine it. "That's dedication."

"Obsession is the word I would use," Max states.

"Unfortunately, I think Max is right," Beatrix admits. "Charlotte often included the legend of King Arthur in her work in some form or other. She had hundreds of sketch books. She'd paint Excalibur, or a knight in shining armour, or the Round Table, or Merlin. She often copied works of art. One of her best was a copy of John Garrick's painting called *The Death of King Arthur.*"

"I know it," I whisper. It portrays a mortally wounded Arthur lying in the arms of one of his knights, I'm not sure which, maybe Bedevere, as the ship arrives through the mists to carry him away to the Isle of Avalon.

I look up at Arthur. He's frowning, and he doesn't look at me.

I turn my attention back to the painting. "What's that?" I point to a strange black shape at the bottom. It's tall and thin, made of criss-crossing black lines.

"Have you heard of the painting by Hans Holbein the Younger, called *The Ambassadors*?" Beatrix asks. Arthur and I shake our heads. "It's a painting of two men from the Tudor period, surrounded by lots of inanimate objects. It also contains a skull in something called anamorphic perspective—you can't see it properly unless you look at the painting from a particular angle."

Slowly, she lifts the bottom of the painting until we're almost looking at it flat. And suddenly there, at the bottom, the black lines seem to magically move and form a new shape.

It's a triquetra, and beneath it are the letters M and S.

I've seen it before. The women who were friends of the murdered Valerie Hopkins-Brown had a tattoo of it on the inside of their wrists. There's only one thing I can deduce from this.

Charlotte Small is a member of the coven called Morgana's Sisters. And that means she is a witch.

Chapter Three

"Dinner's ready," I say briskly, turning away to fiddle with the starters. "We'll talk about it more in a minute. If you'd like to sit up at the dining table, I'll bring it in. Arthur, can you serve the wine please? It's on the table."

"Of course," he says.

Taking the painting with them, Beatrix and Max leave the kitchen, heading for the other end of the long living room, which houses my grandmother's old oak dining table and six chairs.

Arthur waits a moment, then slips an arm around my waist. "Are you all right?" he murmurs.

I nod, concentrating on tweaking the herbs on top of the salmon and prawns so they're just right. I haven't yet told him that the woman on top of the cliff knew him. I'm oddly afraid, and that's only got worse now Beatrix has revealed that Charlotte is a member of Morgana's Sisters.

He bends and kisses my hair. "Don't worry. We'll work it out."

I give him a quick smile. "I know. It'll be fine."

His shrewd blue eyes study me. He has a way of looking at me as if he can see through the outer shell that everyone else sees, right into my heart.

"You look amazing tonight," he says. He slides a hand into my hair, which is loose, hanging down my back in red waves, and lifts a lock of it, letting it slip through his fingers. "It's so silky." His gaze drops to my mouth. "You're the most beautiful woman I've ever seen."

Heat fills my face. "I think you need your eyesight tested."

His lips curve up a little, but he moves his hand to the back of my head and holds me there as he kisses me.

I sigh, enjoying the movement of his mouth across mine, the scent of his aftershave, just the feel of him close to me. When he eventually lifts his head, I feel a little dizzy with love.

"I'll pour the wine," he says, kisses my forehead, and leaves the room.

I blow out a long breath and pick up two of the plates. I can tell the man was skilled with a sword—he knows exactly how to disarm me!

I take the plates into the dining room, return for the other two, and take my seat. I feel more composed now, the shock of the revelation having sunk in.

"So," I say as Arthur pours some Pinot Gris into my glass, "come on then, tell us more about Charlotte Small."

"Are you sure?" Beatrix eyes me astutely. "I have a feeling I shocked you back there. Would you rather wait until after dinner?"

"No, no, I'm okay. It was the realization that Charlotte was a member of Morgana's Sisters." I clear my throat. "The thing is… I had a vision a few days ago."

Both Max and Beatrix's eyebrows rise. I tell them about the woman on the cliff top, the man who kissed her, and how she fell to her death.

"I was looking through her eyes," I tell them. "For a moment I thought I was seeing the future, and it was me falling. But now… I have a feeling it was Charlotte." I glance at Arthur. "I haven't had a chance to tell you, but I had another vision in the café of a woman standing behind me, the same way I saw Valerie Hopkins-Brown after she'd died. Of course, I don't know what Charlotte looks like, so I don't know if it was her."

"Oh, I can help with that," Beatrix says. She takes her phone out of the handbag by her chair, spends a moment typing something in, then turns it around to show me. "This is my art class at the local studio a few months ago. We had an exhibition. Charlotte's there, on the right. Is that who you saw?"

I'm shocked, and yet somehow at the same time also not surprised, to see the shortish woman in her mid-thirties, this time dressed in baggy jeans and a T-shirt that's too tight. Her blonde hair is drawn back into a ponytail, but it's definitely her. I swallow hard and nod.

"So that confirms it," Arthur says. "The woman in your vision was Charlotte Small. She went missing on Friday, and it seems she's probably dead, pushed over the cliff by the man you saw." He meets my gaze for a moment, frowning, as if he can sense I'm keeping something back. But he just looks across at Beatrix and says, "What was she like as a person?"

Beatrix has a mouthful of her starter and chews as she thinks. "This is very good," she tells me. "Lovely fresh flavours." She has a mouthful of wine. "She was an oddball. A good artist. I didn't know she was a witch, obviously." She hesitates. "I don't want to be mean... but she wasn't very well liked in the group. I always encourage everyone to be complimentary about each other's work; it's so easy to knock someone's confidence, and anyway, we're all about self-expression, not producing the next Monet. But she could be cruel to the others in the group. She didn't seem to have many friends."

"Do you have any idea who the man was that you saw her with?" Max asks me.

"No. I didn't recognize him."

"Her husband?"

"Definitely not her husband," I say vehemently. "She was having an affair with him."

"How strange that she was also a member of Morgana's Sisters," Beatrix says.

I push a prawn around my plate. "I'm not sure it's a coincidence."

Arthur leans back in his chair, turning his wine glass in his fingers. "What do you mean?"

"Well... in my vision... as Charlotte was falling, thoughts flashed through her mind of the man who kissed her. She was thinking, 'I thought he loved me. But he was just using me to get what he wanted.' And then..." I sneak a glance at Arthur. He's looking at me the way I look at Merlin when he steals one of my socks. I drop my gaze. "In her mind, she said, 'I think of Arthur and the part I've played in his downfall.' She felt regret, but it was too late for her to do anything about it."

"You should have told me," Arthur says quietly as I continue to push the prawn around with my fork.

"I don't know why I didn't," I admit. "I was... frightened."

"Understandably so," Beatrix soothes. "It's all very unnerving."

"Why do you think Charlotte's husband hasn't reported her as missing?" Max asks.

"Maybe he knew she was having an affair," Beatrix replies. "He could have thought she'd run away or something."

The details of the vision are coming back to me now I'm allowing myself to dwell on them. "I've just remembered—one of the thoughts going through her head as she kissed the man was that they were nearly free. She referred to having placed some stones, and because they were all done, she was convinced the man was going to propose. She actually took off her wedding ring there and dropped it on the ground."

"What stones?" Max asks.

"I don't know." My stomach churns uneasily. "It sounds as if Charlotte knew something about Arthur. And 'he was just using me to get what he wanted' tells me that the guy on the cliff top used her to discover what she knew, until he didn't need her anymore."

We fall silent for a moment, thinking about the implications of that.

"What should we do?" Max asks eventually. "Should we report Charlotte as missing? How do we prove that we know she's been murdered?"

"We can't," Beatrix says. "But you can talk to Immi and at least forewarn her."

My best friend is the DCI at our local police station. She's aware I'm a witch, and it wouldn't be the first time I've used witchcraft to help her solve a crime.

"I'll call her after dinner," I tell them.

"Yes," Beatrix replies. "We should concentrate on the meal, because it's absolutely delicious, as usual."

"Lovely," Max agrees, finishing off a piece of salmon. "Perfect for the time of year."

Arthur's already finished his, so I know he enjoyed it. "I'm glad you all like it," I say, rather shyly. My appetite has faded away, but I force myself to finish the starter while Arthur and Max tell us about the work they've done today.

Afterward, I serve up the chicken pot pie with the roasted vegetables, and the others carefully keep the talk away from Charlotte Small and the painting. Underneath the table, though, Merlin comes to sit on my foot and rests his head on my knee, so I know he can sense my unease. He saw Charlotte's ghost earlier. I'm convinced he knows there's something going on here, despite Arthur's statement that Merlin can only see mist. *He's a bit confused*, he said. Usually it's Merlin who alerts us to the fact that someone has been murdered. Why was it me who found out this time?

We finish off the meal with an orange upside-down cake with crème fraîche. Arthur loves citrus fruit—oranges, lemons, grapefruit. They were introduced into England probably around the time of the

Crusades, so although he was used to cherries, berries, apples, and plums, he hadn't tried any of the exotic fruit now available.

I eat a little of the cake, half-listening to Beatrix talking about a commission she received from a couple to paint Glastonbury Abbey, but it's hard to concentrate, and my mind keeps wandering, thinking about Charlotte. I think about the Queen of Cups Tarot card, the waves crashing on the shore. The Queen represents a woman with a big imagination, maybe psychic, and would fit Charlotte, as she was apparently a witch. She was creative, intuitive, and artistic. She was probably a water sign—Cancer, Scorpio, or Pisces.

She was a Scorpio. It comes to me suddenly. Scorpios can have many good characteristics, but they can also be jealous, secretive, and resentful. If she was born at dawn, it would mean her rising sign was also Scorpio, or maybe she had one or more of the major planets also in that sign, which would emphasize its traits.

She was obsessed with Arthur. Maybe not the real man as I know him, but the legend of the once and future king, the mythical figure who bore a strange connection to the land of England. The Green Man, the Oak King, who flourished in the summer and died in the winter, only to be reborn again the next spring. An ancient heritage going back thousands of years, to the first people who came to this land. The builders of Stonehenge and Amesbury, those who understood nature, and for whom life was an unending cycle of life, death, and rebirth…

"Gwen!"

I blink and focus, seeing them all staring at me with concern.

"Are you okay?" Beatrix asks cautiously. "You zoned out."

"She did that after she had her vision," Arthur says.

"I'm okay." I shake off the strange misgivings that seem determined to drag me down and rise from the table. "Come on, drinks in the living room." I begin to pick up the plates.

"We'll do that," Beatrix says. "Why don't you go and ring Immi? I get the feeling it might make you feel better."

I hesitate. "Are you sure?"

"That's the rule," Max says cheerfully. "The host does the cooking; the guests do the clearing up."

"I'll help," Arthur says, picking up some plates. He glances at me as he passes, concern in his eyes, but he doesn't say anything.

Giving in, I find my mobile and go to the other end of the room, where the sofa and chairs face the TV and the log fire that's crackling in the grate. It might be May, but it'll be a while yet before it's too warm for a fire in the evening, and besides, I find it comforting.

In the kitchen, I can hear the murmur of voices and the clatter of plates as the others begin to wash the dishes. I know they're talking about me, and why I went into a trance. I can't explain it. All I know is that Arthur and I are connected to Charlotte, and it's making me very uneasy.

I pull up Imogen's number, press dial, and wait for her to answer.

Chapter Four

It takes about ten rings for Imogen to answer. I'm just about to hang up when I hear a somewhat breathless, "Hello?"

"It's me," I say, trying not to laugh. "Sorry, did I interrupt something?"

Imogen has been dating Christian Wheeler from the museum for over a month now. They've taken it slow, mostly because Imogen is super busy with her job as a detective chief inspector, but also because she's been hurt badly before. Christian is obviously aware of that, and he wanted to make sure she was ready before they took their relationship to the next level.

Which, by the tone of her voice, they were just in the process of doing.

"We're making out on the sofa," Imogen informs me, then laughs.

I grin. "I can feel Christian rolling his eyes. Do you want to call me later?"

"No, he can wait. He can get us both a drink," she says. In the background, Christian grumbles, but I know he's only teasing her. The two of them have a delightful relationship. I'm so pleased for her. And I'm only a little jealous.

"Everything all right?" Imogen asks.

"Yes… But I thought I ought to let you know about something."

"Oh? Not another murder?" She's teasing, but when I don't reply she says, "Oh no, seriously?"

"Maybe. I had a vision back on the first of May of a woman being pushed over a cliff. I thought it was just a dream, but then I saw her ghost today in a reflection." Imogen has been with me when I've had visions before, so I know she will believe me. "And then tonight Beatrix came over for dinner, and she told me that one of her art students has apparently been missing since Friday. She showed me her picture—it's the same woman."

"Wow. Who is it?"

"Her name is Charlotte Small. Mid-thirties. Married, although not happily by the sound of it. Her husband hasn't reported her missing."

"You think he's done away with her?"

"No, I don't think so. In my vision, she was kissing a man, and it sounded as if they were having an affair. She was talking about how they'd both be free soon, and she was hoping he'd propose to her, but he pushed her over the cliff."

"Some proposal."

"Yeah."

"Hmm. Thank you." There's a clink of ice in a glass, so I know Christian is handing her a drink, probably a Cognac, knowing Immi. "By the way," she continues, "I saw something interesting today."

"Oh?"

"I called in at Perry's Bookshop in town to pick up a book I'd ordered for Christian."

Leah Perry was one of the suspects I interviewed when Valerie Hopkins-Brown was murdered. She's also a member of Morgana's Sisters.

"She had a bandage around her left wrist," Imogen says. "I asked her if she'd done something to her arm, and she told me she'd had a tattoo removed."

My eyebrows rise. "Really? I wonder if that means she's left the coven?"

"Possibly. I didn't like to ask, but I thought you might like to know."

"Yes, that's very interesting."

"Well, I don't have any other news," Imogen says.

I smile. "I'd better let you go. I'm sure you have better things to be doing than talking to me."

She gives a delightfully girlish giggle. "Yes I have. That's very true."

"Are you naked yet?"

"Gwen! You wicked woman."

"I'm living vicariously. I expect you to give me all the deets tomorrow in great detail."

She laughs. "Still waiting for Arthur to make a move, are you?"

I sigh and glance at the door. I can still hear him in the kitchen, talking to Max. "I know I said I needed time, but if I send out any more signals, planes are going to start landing in the back garden."

"Take your clothes off in front of him. That normally helps."

"Do you know, I'd try that, but I'm worried he's just going to stare at me and then gently ask me to get dressed again." I say it in a light-hearted tone, but Imogen doesn't laugh.

"You really don't think he'd leap on you?" she asks curiously.

"No, I don't. And I don't know why, which is even more disturbing. He couldn't be any more loving. And we've kissed an awful lot. But he's holding back, I can feel it." Unusually for me, tears prick my eyelids and my throat tightens.

"Aw," Imogen says. "There will be a very good reason for it, I know there will."

"I'm not so sure." I sniff.

"Rubbish. He can't take his eyes off you when you're in the room. Christian said that when he took him to that football match, Arthur talked about you non-stop. He's crazy about you. He loves you, Gwen. He's waited fifteen hundred years for you. And he's old-fashioned. He comes from a time when matches were made between rival warlords, and men had to wait until they married to even kiss their bride. It's possible he's a bit out of his depth."

"Hmm. I don't think he's lacking in experience. I'm sure I wasn't the only woman in his life back then. He was hardly a monk."

"I'm sure he wasn't. He looks like a red-blooded male. Just like Christian." Her boyfriend snorts in the background. "But you're not just a woman he wants to have a bit of fun with. You're the one, Gwen. He's waited for you. He doesn't want to rush this. He wants it to be perfect."

"I suppose I just need to wait. But I feel so…" I sigh.

"Yeah, tell me about it," she replies. "Christian told me if we don't go all the way soon, I'm going to melt him with my lustful laser eyes."

That makes me laugh. "I'd better leave you to it, then. Have fun."

"I'll do my best. Oh, Gwen?"

"Yes?"

"I'll call Charlotte's husband tomorrow, okay? I'll let you know what I find out."

"Thanks, Immi. Goodnight." I hang up the phone.

I should go into the kitchen and help the others, but I sit for a moment, trying to summon the energy. I feel listless and lethargic. It's unusual for me. I normally have tons of energy and find it difficult to sit still and do nothing. Merlin is in the living room with me, and he comes over and sits on my foot, a sure sign that he's picking up on my agitation.

I'm worried. I don't know why, or what about. Again, that's unusual for me. I don't stress over airy-fairy things, and I consider myself practical and down-to-earth, despite being a witch. I realize then that I haven't meditated for a while, so perhaps I need to ground myself, to re-anchor back to the earth.

I pull the Tarot pack toward me, take the cards out, and shuffle them. I cut them in two and put the lower half on top of the upper half. Then I turn over the top card.

There are seventy-eight cards in the Tarot. There are four suits, similar to a normal deck of playing cards, except these are cups, pentacles, swords, and wands, and instead of a Jack, King, and Queen, there are four 'court' cards—a page, knight, queen, and king. These fifty-six cards symbolize people or everyday issues. Added to these are the twenty-two Major Arcana, which depict bigger, even life-changing events.

The card I've drawn is the Moon—number eighteen of the Major Arcana. A dog and a wolf sit between two standing stones, in front of a lake, howling at the moon. It's a beautiful, magical picture. I study it, my eyelids dropping to half-mast as my breathing deepens and slows. Nothing looks the same in moonlight. The world is full of light and shadows. Colour bleaches to black and white. The shadows hide secrets, things not yet revealed. The Goddess watches over me, but she's hiding her face, subdued, wary. It's spring, so she's the maiden, the crescent moon, young, inexperienced, and innocent, even naive. The Horned God stands in the darkness, watching her, and green vines creep along the ground, ready to pull her down into the earth. Seduction, rich and ripe and sensual and dark. Charlotte had no idea what he was doing, and what would happen to her…

"Gwen!"

My eyes fly open. Arthur has dropped to his haunches in front of me; Beatrix and Max stand to one side, their faces filled with concern. Merlin's brown eyes are fixed on me. Somehow, I know he's aware of the things I can see and feel.

"What?" I say.

"You've been sitting like that for ten minutes," Arthur says. "We couldn't wake you."

I blink and look at Beatrix. She's calm, but I can see the worry in her eyes.

"I'm all right," I say, returning my gaze to Arthur. "I drew the Moon card, and it gave me a sort of vision… Nothing concrete, just a feeling there are things we aren't aware of yet. Hidden secrets. Charlotte was involved, but she didn't know it all. I think we should be worried about the man she was with, Arthur. He's no ordinary guy. I think he means us harm."

We're all silent for a moment. Then Beatrix says briskly, "Well there's nothing we can do about it now. Let's have a coffee, and then Max and I will leave you to get a good night's sleep."

So we drink coffee in the living room around the fire, as Arthur and Max recount funny stories about some of the guys they work with. The rich earthy smell and taste of coffee always grounds me, and soon I feel normal again, and the shadows retreat back to where they belong.

Eventually, Beatrix declares it's time for them to go, and they head out. We wave goodbye, standing in the doorway like any ordinary couple. It's raining, and to my relief the clouds have covered the moon.

Arthur, Merlin, and I go back into the living room, and Arthur pours us both a small glass of wine, while I watch the rain hammering on the windows, glad to be safe inside.

We sit together on the sofa while Merlin stretches out in front of the fire. I left some change on the table earlier, and Arthur picks up a pound coin, then moves it from his left hand into his right. He blows on his fingers and reveals that the coin has mysteriously vanished. Finally, he reaches behind my ear and produces it.

"Aw," I say, "you'd make a great dad."

He laughs and kisses my forehead. "That's the plan."

I blush. "Show me how you did it?"

"Come here then." He goes through the steps of how to pretend to move the coin from one hand to another until I can do it smoothly.

"You never know when it might come in handy," he says. "How are you feeling now?"

"Okay. Better, thanks."

"Do you want to talk about it?"

I shrug. "Not much to say, really. You know most of it. Charlotte obviously has a connection with us. She regretted playing a part in what she called your downfall. Other than that, I can't tell you much more."

"You're upset," he murmurs, stroking my hair.

I sip my wine. "I just felt we were getting somewhere, you know? And then this happens and throws a spanner in the works."

I don't want to say that I feel it's interrupted the intimacy that was developing between us. I can't put my finger on why.

Arthur takes my glass and puts it on the coffee table with his. Then he pulls me onto his lap, into his arms, and kisses me.

With a rush of relief and joy, I slide my arms around his neck and tilt my head so he can deepen the kiss. He does so, and for a few moments he envelops me in his embrace. Outside, the wind throws the rain at the glass, but inside it's warm, the room filled with the glow from the fire, and Arthur's mouth is hot on mine. His fingers slip beneath my sweater, lingering on my back. My body stirs, like a cat waking up after a long sleep. The thought of exploring Arthur in bed under the cosy duvet gives me goose bumps, and I lift my head to look into his eyes.

Gathering every ounce of courage I possess, like scooping a hundred marbles up in my hands, I say breathlessly, "Will you come to bed with me?"

I wait for his eyes to light up, for a smile to spread across his face.

But instead, a frown mars his forehead, and he says, "It's not the right time."

I move back a little. "What do you mean?"

He hesitates. "I don't know."

"What do you mean, you don't know?"

"I can't explain it, Gwen. I'm sorry."

We study each other for a moment. I'm embarrassed and disappointed. Doesn't he understand how much I want him?

I swallow hard. Anger and hurt sear through me. But it's not my way to give into negative emotions.

I do get to my feet and turn away, though.

He stands, catches my arm, and turns me to face him.

"I'm sorry," he says. He looks genuinely upset, but it doesn't help, because I don't understand.

"Have you changed your mind?" I ask as calmly as I can. "About being with me?"

He looks pained. "No, of course not."

"You can't say that Arthur. You can't say 'of course not' as if it's obvious just seconds after turning me down."

He catches my face in his hands. "I love you, Gwen. I want to be with you."

"But you don't want me in that way?"

A flicker of amusement crosses his face. "I do. Intensely. More than you can imagine."

The heat in his eyes is reassuring, but I still don't understand. "Then—"

He looks away, out into the dark night. "I think it might be something to do with Charlotte Small."

My heart misses a beat. "You mean... you think you knew her?" Thoughts flit through my head—she was a lover of his in his previous life, and now he's torn between the two of us...

But he shakes his head. "No. I'm sure I didn't know her. But ever since you had your first vision of her, I've felt... odd. Distracted. As if I can constantly see something moving out of the corner of my eye."

He puts his arms around me and presses his lips on the top of my hair. I rest my cheek on his chest and close my eyes. "Every day that I'm here, I grow stronger," he states. "I feel more connected, more real, if you like. This is nothing to worry about. I'm not going anywhere."

I don't reply. He's trying to comfort me, but they're platitudes. He doesn't know he's here to stay.

Surely I haven't finally found the man of my dreams, only to lose him again so soon?

Chapter Five

The next day, around eleven a.m., Imogen calls me.

"Got a minute?" she asks.

I'm in the middle of making a batch of mini cakes with a new recipe that Delia and I have come up with. She commented that both she and Melissa suffer from migraines and suggested that some kind of cake or muffin to help headaches might be a good idea. Together, we came up with a Mini Minty Magic Cake using mint leaves from my herb garden, blessed with a simple spell to aid relaxation and pain relief. But it's nothing that won't wait for five minutes, so I say, "Sure," put the bowl aside, and walk through the café and out into the quiet May morning with my phone.

The rain eased over the night, and now everywhere is clean and sparkling. The lawn in front of the abbey is a rich green, and the amber stones look as if someone has scrubbed and polished them. I sit on one of the outside chairs, breathing in the fresh air.

"Thought I'd tell you that I spoke to Jim Small," Imogen says. "Charlotte's husband."

"Oh? And?"

"Very odd customer. I said I'd heard that his wife hadn't been seen for a few days. He told me she was probably off with her fancy man and he didn't give a…" Imogen clears her throat. "It rhymes with 'dying duck.'"

"Goodness."

"I know," Imogen says, "I mean, I understand that he would be angry if he discovered she was having an affair, but you'd think he would still be concerned about her welfare. Anyway, it makes it more difficult for me."

"You can't log her as missing because of that?"

"It's tricky. We divide missing persons into low, medium, and high risk. Forgetting for a moment that you've had the vision of Charlotte, all we know is that she didn't turn up for her art class, and that she hasn't been seen for a few days."

"So that makes her low risk?"

"Well, typically over three hundred thousand people go missing every year in the UK."

My eyes nearly fall out of my head. "How many?"

"I know. Sixty-six percent of them are under eighteen. We assess each case and decide whether the disappearance is out of character. Jim said Charlotte has gone missing before, a few years ago, after they had an argument. She vanished for six days before he discovered that she was in a B&B in the Lake District."

"So it's understandable why Jim's not too concerned," I say.

"Mm. Out of all missing persons cases, only nought-point-six percent of people are found dead. And it's harder to find adults, especially if they don't want to be found."

"But we know that Charlotte did not disappear of her own volition," I point out.

"*We* know that, yes."

I know what she's trying to say. She can hardly report Charlotte as missing because of my vision.

"I'm going to do some sniffing around," Imogen adds. "Obviously, we have Beatrix's report that Charlotte didn't turn up for her art class. I'll try to track down her family and friends and see if anyone else has concerns, but I'm busy at the moment; I'm not sure how much time I can devote to it."

"I understand. Is it okay if I do a little digging?" I ask.

"I was hoping you'd say that." I can hear her smile. "Dig away." She tells me Charlotte's address. "Let me know what you come up with."

"Will do, Immi. Thank you. Oh, before you go—how was last night?"

"Superb," she says. "The man is a god. I've got a permanent smirk on my face this morning."

I chuckle. "I'm so pleased for you."

"No advancement for you?" she asks lightly.

I push a stone across the pavement with my toe. "No. I tried last night, but Arthur turned me down."

"Oh, Gwen, no…"

"It's okay," I add hastily, not sure I can bear her pity. "He insists he's still interested. I think it's something to do with this new case. I'm worried that Charlotte has done some kind of spell on him. He's not himself."

"Hmm. Well, let me know if there's anything I can do. I'll definitely see if I can get one of the lads to spare some time to check her out."

"Thanks, Immi. Speak to you later." I hang up.

I go back inside the café and return to making the Mini Minty Magic Cakes, then after that do a couple of batches of muffins and some more jumbo sausage rolls, as most of the ones I made earlier have sold. But all the while I'm thinking about Charlotte, planning out what I'm going to do later.

At two o'clock, I look up to see that Arthur has come into the café and is standing talking to Cooper.

My heart misses a beat, as it always does when I see him. He's been out with Max today, working on a new housing estate on the outskirts of town. Max has placed him with one of his carpenters, who's been teaching Arthur some modern techniques and how to use the more complicated equipment.

He's wearing jeans, a navy shirt, and his black jacket. On the front of the jacket is a brooch in the shape of a bear. It's a copy of one that Guinevere gave to him in the sixth century for their fifth wedding anniversary. The museum was kind enough to allow me to borrow the original, and I had a copy made by James Mackenzie, owner of the jewellery shop in town, as he didn't want to damage the original. Arthur loves it, and he wears it all the time on his jacket.

Delia's sister, Melissa, has started working for me full-time, so I've been spending the afternoons I'm not at the field unit with Arthur. We've gone to the cinema and local art galleries, driven to look at neighbouring towns like Wells, Taunton, and Yeovil, and spent time shopping and just generally getting him used to life in the twenty-first century.

So far, he's not been that keen to visit historical sites. He seems to have mixed feelings about his previous life and prefers to stay grounded in the present day, so I haven't pushed him.

I wash my hands, grab my jacket from the break room, and go out to meet him. His smile is warm, and he pulls me into his arms for a big hug as I walk up to him.

"Hey, you," I say, thinking how gorgeous he looks in his tight jeans and the thin sweatshirt that stretches across his muscular arms.

"Hey." He bends his head and kisses me, lingering just long enough to bring heat to my face. When he eventually moves back, I see Cooper grinning from ear to ear, and I stick my tongue out at him.

"Come on." I grab Arthur's hand and lead him out to the sound of Cooper's chuckle. "We've got things to do this afternoon."

"Connected with Charlotte?" he asks as we collect Merlin from outside and head off to my car.

"Yes." I tell him what Imogen said, and finish with, "So I thought we could go and have a chat to Jim."

"Great idea. Even if he doesn't think she's missing, he might be able to give us some clues as to where to go next."

"That was my thinking." We get to the car, and I dangle the keys in front of him. "Want to drive?"

"Sure." He takes the keys and gets in the driver's side while I open the back door for Merlin, then stick on the L plates. Arthur heads off, taking the road to Wells, as Charlotte lives on the outskirts.

Getting his licence was tricky considering he didn't have a passport or a birth certificate. I'd known I was going to have to get over that hurdle eventually. I didn't really want to buy a fake one as I thought that could lead to more trouble, and besides apparently they're very expensive, and I don't have that kind of money.

I'm a witch, and therefore it made sense to find a magical solution. Until fairly recently, the only magic I'd done was with my baking, but after the advancements I'd made with the crystal ball and the visions I'd had with Valerie Hopkins-Brown, I thought that maybe my talents were wider than I'd previously understood.

So I spent some time reading through my family's Books of Shadows, and eventually tracked down an intricate confusion spell that Josephine, my great-great-grandmother, had invented by using rosemary, which aids the memory, and reading a spell out backward to reverse the effect. I adapted it a bit, scattered the passport application with the blessed herb, and read my newly created spell out backward, asking the person who dealt with Arthur's application to believe they'd seen his birth certificate. Shortly afterward, we got his passport through the post, following which we were able to apply for his provisional driving licence.

Since then, he's been driving Max to work in his car when he comes to pick him up, and he often drives my little Suzuki. I love driving, but I don't mind sharing with Arthur while he learns the ropes. He's pretty good at it, although—like now—he occasionally misses third gear and the car protests with a loud grinding noise.

"Oops," he says, finding fifth gear hurriedly. "Sorry."

I laugh. "It's okay. You're doing really well."

"It's a lot harder than riding a horse."

"I'm surprised. Horses have a mind of their own. Cars don't."

"But you create a bond with your horse that doesn't happen with a car."

"Yes it does," I protest, patting the Suzuki's dashboard. "I've had this little sweetie a long time."

Arthur gives me a fond smile. "Have you ever been horse riding?"

"No. Couldn't afford it when I was younger." I glance across curiously. "Did I used to ride?"

"All the time," he says. "We both did. I had to move around a lot with the army, and you always came with me. You refused to stay at home." He gives a wistful smile, and for a moment I'm sure he's not seeing the road but is instead peering back into the misty past.

I look out of the side window. I wish I could remember my previous life. I only have his word to go on that we were once married and in love. I'd like to have his memories of us together. I feel that it might reassure me more that things are going to work out in this lifetime.

"Hey." He takes my hand. "Why so sad?"

I shrug and give him a small smile. "No reason."

He brushes across the back of my hand with his thumb. "You know I'm crazy about you, right?"

I look across at him, and for a moment his blue eyes bore into mine before he returns his gaze to the road. "I'm sorry," he murmurs, "I shouldn't refer to our previous life together. I know it unsettles you, and it's not fair."

"I just wish I could remember it, too."

"I know. But what we've got to concentrate on is that this life is going to be even better than our first one together. Who knows what exciting things the future holds?"

His words give me hope. He told me a while ago that I'd had some miscarriages in my previous incarnation, and that we'd been unable to have children. Hopefully, we can correct that in this lifetime.

Marriage, love, and a family. I can barely dare to hope.

We navigate our way to a new housing estate on the edge of Wells. "Here we go." Arthur indicates and pulls over on the side of the road in front of a terraced house. He turns off the engine, and we all get out, Merlin included, and walk through the garden gate up the small path to the front door.

It doesn't look very well-tended; weeds have run riot, crowding out the straggly flowers. There's rubbish on the tiny front lawn—bricks, a broken hose, an old rusted bicycle. The doorstep needs a scrub. Clearly, Charlotte and Jim aren't house-proud.

We ring the bell. There's no reply.

"Maybe he's out," Arthur says.

Disappointed, I ring it again. This time, we hear footsteps inside, and then the door opens.

A man glares at us. He's probably only late thirties, but he looks older, with dark shadows under his eyes and his scruffy hair threaded with grey. His clothes are rumpled, and he smells unwashed. His sweater bears an egg stain.

"What?" he demands.

"Mr. Small?" I ask. "I'm so sorry to bother you, but I was wondering whether you've heard from Charlotte?"

"No," he snaps. "I haven't. And who are you? I haven't seen you before."

"I'm in Charlotte's art class." I cross my fingers behind my back to ward off the lie. "It's unusual for her not to come to the studio. I thought I'd just check that she's okay."

He shoves his hands in his pockets. "I've no idea where she is." He's angry, but I can also see hurt beneath his frustration.

"My name's Gwen, and this is Arthur," I tell him. "Could we come in for a moment? If you could tell us a little about her, maybe we'll be able to track her down?"

He stares at me, and I'm sure he's going to refuse. Then, to my surprise, he mutters, "Whatever," and he walks away, leaving the door open.

Chapter Six

I hesitate as to whether I should leave Merlin outside, but the Labradoodle trots inside after Arthur, so I shrug and follow them in. I close the door behind us, and Jim leads us into his living room.

The table is stacked with dirty dishes, and beer bottles litter the area around his armchair. Several weeks' worth of dust coats the TV table, and fluff and bits of dropped food and rubbish speckle the carpet.

"Coffee?" he grunts.

I don't particularly want to consume anything in this house, but it might give us more time to question him, so I nod, and reluctantly Arthur follows my cue. Jim goes through to the kitchen, and soon we hear the clatter of spoons and the whistle of the kettle.

Arthur looks around him, then at me. The look on his face makes me fight not to giggle. Merlin sneezes, which suggests he's also trying not to laugh.

"Shh," I scold, moving some dirty laundry from the sofa to a chair so the two of us can sit.

We perch on the edge, unwilling to sink into the cushions because we're not sure what may be hiding between or beneath them. Luckily, it's not long before Jim reappears. Surprisingly, he has a tray with three mugs, a milk jug, and a sugar bowl, as if he's serving afternoon tea to the queen. He stumbles a little as he places the tray, though, causing the coffee to slop over the edge.

"Thank you." I take one of the mugs. It has a stain around the rim.

I spoon some sugar into my mug. Jim adds several spoonfuls and a large splash of milk, stirs it, and sits back in his chair. He looks exhausted, with heavy bags under his eyes. He doesn't look well.

"Thank you for inviting us in," I say gently. "I'm hoping we can find out a little about Charlotte. I'm worried something's happened to her."

He snorts and has a mouthful of coffee. "She's just fine, off with her fancy man up north somewhere, I'm sure."

I blow on my coffee. "You think Charlotte was having an affair?"

"I know she was."

"How?" Arthur asks. "Have you seen her with a man?"

Jim shakes his head. "She's been different, that's all."

"In what way?" I ask. I go to sip the coffee, then stop at the last minute as I see Merlin watching me. He can see how dirty the mug is. I put it down without tasting it. Arthur hasn't even picked his up.

Jim shrugs. "Tarting herself up. Wearing makeup, perfume, that kind of thing. Buying new clothes. Going out all hours of the day and night. She'd come home smelling of him. It was disgusting." He looks out of the window, his expression thunderous. He's jealous; clearly, he still has feelings for her. Or maybe it's just a dog-in-the-manger thing—she's his wife, and even though he doesn't want her, he doesn't want anyone else to have her.

"How long has this been going on?" I ask.

"A month. Maybe two." He blows out a long breath. "Yes, more like two. Back in March, something happened to her. She started being all secretive, going in her studio and staying there for hours. Sometimes I'd go in, and she'd be working on her charts—all those hundreds of figures. Never could work it out."

"Charts?" Arthur queries.

"Yeah, you know, the stars and stuff."

For a moment I think he's talking about celebrities, but Arthur says, "You mean astrology?" and Jim nods.

"She likes horoscopes," he says.

I wonder if it's a coincidence that Mary Paxton used The Star Sign Spell to bind Liza Banks's spirit to this plane when she died. Maybe it's something they teach in their coven.

"Have you heard her talk about something called Morgana's Sisters?" I ask. It doesn't surprise me when he shakes his head. It's quite common for witches to keep their practices secret from their family, especially if they think their partners will laugh at them.

"What did she do for a living?" I query.

"She worked at the council," he says. "Housing department."

"Does she have any close friends?" Arthur asks.

"That's something else weird," Jim replies. "She and Anita Finley had been best friends since high school. But they must have had a bust up, because Anita stopped coming around, and Charlotte refused to talk about her."

"Hmm. So you don't know who Charlotte was having an affair with, if indeed she was having an affair?" I ask him. He shakes his head again.

"Anyway, what's this all about?" he asks suddenly. "Why do you care what's happened to her?"

"I'm worried about her," I tell him. "I think something might have happened to her, and I'd like to make sure she's safe."

I can tell by the look on his face that he's suspicious that somebody might care about his wife. I get the feeling that not many people liked Charlotte, and he's unused to anyone taking an interest in her.

"We think you should report her as missing," I urge.

His face takes on a stubborn, resolute look. "A police officer rang me this morning, asking about Charlotte. I told her I didn't think she'd gone missing. Last time she took off, I panicked for days, but she was living the life of Riley up in the Lake District. So I'm not going to change my mind now. I'll look like a real idiot."

That makes me bristle. "Is that important, if your wife really is in danger?"

He glares at me. I glare back.

Arthur clears his throat. "I wonder whether it would be possible for us to take a look at your wife's studio?"

"What for?" Jim snaps.

"We might be able to find a clue as to where she is," Arthur replies calmly. "You seem like a good man at heart, Jim. I understand that you're upset at the thought of your wife having an affair—what man wouldn't be? But I know you wouldn't want anything to happen to her."

Jim studies his slippers. Arthur has outmanoeuvred him. He can hardly say now that he doesn't care if she's missing.

He looks up at me then. His eyes are unfocussed, and his skin has taken on a grey, greasy look. I frown.

"Room next to the back door," he says sullenly.

"Thank you." Arthur rises and holds out his hand to me. I take it, and he pulls me to my feet, then leads me out of the living room and down the hallway, Merlin trotting along behind. At the end is the back door to the garden. To the left is the kitchen; on the right is a closed door to another room.

For a moment, I wonder whether Charlotte has locked it, but to my surprise the handle turns in Arthur's hand. He opens it, and we go inside.

It's a small room—these new terraced houses are tiny. As it's next to the kitchen, it could have been a small dining room, but she's converted it into a kind of studio. In front of the window is an easel and a table with watercolour paints and palettes. On the other side is a desk with a computer and a tray stacked with sheets of paper filled with handwritten numbers.

"Astrology?" Arthur asks, coming to look with me.

I nod and shuffle through the papers, expecting to see birth charts of her friends, family, and work colleagues. "That's weird. These aren't birth charts."

"What are they?"

I don't answer for a moment as I study the lists of figures. They're neatly drawn in columns, with planetary alignments on the left corresponding to two sets of numbers on the right. "These are lines of longitude and latitude."

"Like on a map?"

"Exactly." There's a large map of the United Kingdom pinned to the wall behind the table, and we turn our attention to it. There are about two hundred push-pins marking locations on the map. I check one of the sets of longitude and latitude on the sheet of figures and locate it on the map. Yes, there's a pin right there, in a place called Caerleon in South Wales.

"It's a Roman legionary fort," I tell Arthur.

"Oh?"

"Some scholars also think it's a possible site for the location of Camelot," I add.

We study each other for a long moment. Then we both look back at the map.

"Do you recognize any more of the locations?" Arthur asks.

I examine them. They're scattered all across the UK. "This is Winchester, where a medieval copy of the Round Table hangs on the wall." I move my hand to north-west Wales. "This is Dinas Emrys, where Merlin was born, and where two dragons fought—one white, one red. The red dragon won and became the national symbol of Wales."

"So… what was Charlotte doing?" Arthur studies one of the sheets of numbers.

"I don't know, but I'm guessing all these sites are connected with the legend of King Arthur in some way." I leave the desk and go over to the table that bears the paints. "Beatrix said Charlotte had hundreds of sketch books. Where do you think they are?"

We look around the room, but there are no boxes, no cabinets that could contain all her sketch books.

"Hmm," I say. "The curious incident of the dog in the nighttime."

Arthur raises an eyebrow. "What?"

"It's from the Sherlock Holmes story, *The Adventure of Silver Blaze*," I reply. Arthur has been reading some of Conan Doyle's short stories lately, so he's aware of the detective. "Holmes is investigating the disappearance of a racehorse. He says to one of the Scotland Yard detectives that it's interesting what the dog did in the nighttime. The detective said the dog did nothing, and Holmes says *that* was the curious incident—the dog didn't make a noise, and therefore it knew the person who took the horse."

"So you're saying it's curious that Charlotte's sketch books aren't here."

"Yes. She's an artist. Beatrix implied she was never without one. So where are they?" I look around in frustration. "I doubt she would have taken them to work."

"Maybe they're in her bedroom?"

"Where Jim could have found them? No, she wouldn't want anyone else looking at them. They must be here."

So we search the room again, taking our time to check every nook and cranny.

It's Arthur who has the idea to look beneath the old rug on the floor. There's no carpet in the room, and beneath the rug, the floorboards are bare. "Score!" he says, his new-found football exclamation from Christian. I run over to him and drop to my knees to look at where he's examining what's clearly a loose floorboard.

Together, we prise up the board and lay it to one side. We lean over and look into the hole. It's maybe three feet square, and it's full of sketch books.

Chapter Seven

I sit on the floorboards and stare at the books. They're all the same—A4 size, with a light-green cover. I've seen them for sale in the bookshop in town.

I pick one up. On the front, in the same writing as the list of numbers, is the date—27 July, 2011. I open it. It's full of sketches. Some of them are pencil drawings, others are watercolours. The pictures are of a variety of things; still life—bottles and fruit and other objects, landscapes, and people, none of whom I recognize. A diary of an artist's life, showing her thoughts and interests of the time.

I slot the book back in the cubby hole and choose one closer to the front. It's dated 15 October 2017. I open it up. The style of these drawings is quite different. By this point, Charlotte had clearly begun studying witchcraft. The drawings are more fantastical and include stylized pentacles, candles, moons, and other witchy paraphernalia, as well as the Morgana's Sisters symbol of a triquetra. I also spot a couple of drawings of knights in shining armour and medieval ladies—maybe the beginning of Charlotte's focus on the Arthurian legend.

I put the book back and flick through other, later ones.

"She's becoming more obsessed," Arthur says as I turn over page after page of paintings that illustrate Arthur and his knights.

I look up and meet his gaze. His eyes are carefully guarded; I can't tell what he's thinking.

Unlike the others, this book has several blank pages at the end, but it's not the last book. I pick up the final book in the hole. The cover is dated March this year, so it must be her most recent. Only the first three pages are filled.

Arthur looks over my shoulder as I study the pages. These aren't fantasy drawings; they're sketches of buildings. The first, which bears a large number one in the top left-hand corner, is a small stone church. The drawing on the next page has the numeral two in the corner and it looks like a hillfort—maybe bronze or Iron Age. Number three depicts the crumbling remains of what appears to be a medieval castle.

"Do you know these places?" Arthur asks.

I shake my head. Charlotte's drawings are good, but I don't recognize the sites from these small snapshots. Still, I get a tingle all the way down my spine, and when I look up, I can tell from the way Merlin's large brown eyes are boring into mine that he also feels that this book is important.

"Do you think Jim will let us borrow it?" I ask.

"Hopefully." Arthur gets to his feet and offers me a hand to help me up.

"We should go." I want to get out of the house, which is heavy with sadness and regret and something else… an uneasy sense of menace. It's almost as if Charlotte is here in the room with us, resentful that we're pawing through her belongings. There are no mirrors here, or I'm sure I would have seen her reflection glaring at me.

We put the floorboard and rug back and return to the living room. "I wonder whether you'd mind if we borrow Charlotte's sketch book," I say to Jim, who's slumped in the chair.

"Whatever," he says. He looks half asleep.

"Are you okay?" I'm reluctant to help this man who I really don't like. No matter what Charlotte has done to him, I find it distasteful that he doesn't seem to care that something might have happened to her. But he doesn't look well, and, despite my better instincts, I'm worried about him.

He nods and swigs from a bottle in his hand. Even though it's only three p.m., he's moved onto beer, and he already seems half-drunk as he stares at the action movie on the TV.

"Come on," Arthur murmurs, and we head out, closing the front door behind us.

I blow out a breath as we return to the car. "What an unpleasant man. No wonder she had an affair."

"Still doesn't make it right," Arthur says, tight-lipped. "She should have left him before she started dating someone else."

"You're right," I say softly. "Nothing condones cheating on a partner."

Arthur has very strong views on it. As we get back into the car, I wonder whether that has something to do with the story about Guinevere and Lancelot. When I first mentioned it, I could see it angered him that the Arthurian legend stated that his wife had had an affair. I suppose if you were devoted to your wife, it must hurt to know that everyone thinks she was unfaithful.

"So what's next?" Arthur starts the engine and carefully pulls away.

"I'm not sure." I look at the sketch book on my lap. "I'll do my best to try and identify the sites she drew. I'd like to find out more about her. We can track down her friend, Anita Finley, and see if she's prepared to talk. The other thing I thought about doing was going to see Leah Perry."

"The bookshop owner?" Arthur raises his eyebrows. "Why so?"

"I completely forgot to tell you," I admit. "When I was talking to Immi last night, she told me she'd seen Leah, and she had a bandage on her wrist. When Immi asked her what she'd done, she said she'd had her tattoo removed."

"Oh… problems in Morgana's Sisters?"

"She must have left the coven," I say. "It'll be very interesting to see if she's willing to talk about it, and what she can tell us about Charlotte."

"Do you want to go now?" he asks. "It's only just after three."

"Okay."

So Arthur heads into town, navigating the roundabout and the traffic lights carefully. He has fun parallel-parking on the road, taking a couple of goes at it, but manages it in the end, and we get out and head for the bookshop.

Leah is behind the till, serving a customer, while her assistant, Casey, dusts the shelves. She smiles at us as we approach.

"Hello you two," she says once the customer leaves. "How are you doing?"

"Good, thank you." I glance around the shop. There are a couple of other customers, and I don't want to be overheard. "Leah, I was wondering whether I could have a word in private?"

Her eyebrows rise. "Oh. What about?"

I glance at the bandage on her left wrist and murmur, "About Morgana's Sisters."

She stares at me for a long moment. Her gaze slides to Arthur. Then she looks across at Casey. "Case, can you cover for me please?"

"Sure." The girl comes over and takes her place behind the counter. Leah gestures with her head for us to follow her, and she leads us to the end of the shop and into a store room.

She switches on the light, pushes the door almost shut, and turns to us with a cautious look. "I don't know what you're talking about," she says.

I frown. "So why did you agree to talk to us?"

"I don't know." She looks scared, and it occurs to me that her coven might have threatened her into keeping quiet.

I decide it's best to be honest. "Leah, I don't know if you're aware, but I'm a witch, too."

Her jaw drops. "I didn't know, no."

"My great-grandmother was invited to be a member of Morgana's Sisters," I inform her, "although she chose not to join. I found out about the coven through one of her Books of Shadows."

She nods, but doesn't say anything, clearly cautious about opening up.

"You know I helped to investigate the deaths of both Liza Banks and Valerie Hopkins-Brown," I continue. "It turns out that both the murderers were members of Morgana's Sisters."

She studies her shoes. "I know."

"Well, it seems that another member of the coven has gone missing. I'm trying to find out what happened to her, and I wondered whether you'd be able to help."

"Who's missing?"

"Her name is Charlotte Small," Arthur says.

Leah blinks. "Never heard of her."

I frown. "Really? I'm sure she's a member. She included the symbol for the coven on one of her drawings."

Leah shrugs. "She's probably a member of another branch."

Arthur and I exchange a startled look. "There's more than one branch?" I ask.

"There are branches all over the country," Leah says.

That shocks me. I'd assumed it was a local group.

"I heard that you'd had your tattoo removed," I say. "Would you be willing to tell me why?"

Leah lifts her arm, examining the bandage that covers the place where her tattoo had been. "If you leave, you have to remove the tattoo," she says.

"You've left Morgana's Sisters?"

She nods.

"May I ask why?"

She shifts uncomfortably. "I can't discuss it with you."

"Charlotte's life might be at stake," I inform her. "I hate to say this, but I'll have to ask the police to bring you in for questioning if you won't talk to me."

She folds her arms and studies the floor. I'm sure she's going to ask us to leave. She thinks for a long time, and I know she must be weighing up the pros and cons of complying.

In the end, she just gives a long sigh. "No," she says. "Don't tell the police. I'll talk. But you mustn't tell anyone where the information came from."

I glance at Arthur. At last, we might be getting somewhere!

"My mother was in the coven," she says. "I started going when I was thirteen." She gives me a curious look. "You're a solitary witch?"

"Yes. A kitchen witch," I clarify. "I mainly do magic through my baking."

"How lovely," she says. "I'm really looking forward to practicing alone. The coven is very prescriptive. Everything has to be done just so, the way the elders instruct. There's a strict hierarchy, and knowledge is closely guarded. Spells and other information are only shared after you've been with the coven a certain length of time, and you have to pass tests."

"That's a shame," I say, thinking of the Books of Shadows I have from the women in my family. Her use of the word 'elders' gets me thinking, too. What with her comment about various branches, the coven sounds much bigger than I expected. It doesn't sound like a group of friends dabbling in herbs and spells. It's much more organized than that.

"It's a very old coven," Leah confirms. "We have records of it going back to the seventeenth century, but everyone thinks it goes back way further than that. We're told that it's called Morgana's Sisters because we follow the same path as Morgana from the Arthurian stories."

"What path is that?" I ask.

"We're taught that she was a powerful witch who had the power to do anything she wanted. You know the Wiccan Rede?"

She means the statement that provides the key moral code in witchcraft. "And it harm none, do what you will?"

She nods. "In 1534, Francois Rabelais wrote 'Do as thou wilt, because men that are free, of gentle birth, well-bred and at home in civilized company possess a natural instinct that inclines them to virtue and saves them from vice.'" She speaks the words by rote—clearly, she's had to say them many times.

"The thing is," she continues, "in Morgana's Sisters, this has come to mean that anything goes. 'Do as thou wilt' has become the central tenet, and they've dropped the 'and it harm none' part. Care of the coven and its members is all that matters. Morgana is pretty much worshipped, and we're all supposed to aspire to be like her—the all-powerful enemy of King Arthur. They're heavily into the legends and see themselves as the antithesis of Arthur and his knights."

I glance at Arthur. His expression is stony.

"After the murders of Liza and Valerie," Leah continues, "it became clear to me that many of the sisters were practicing dark magic. I decided that I wanted out of the coven. It's not easy to leave. They made it very... unpleasant." Her skin has grown pale. I can only imagine what she had to go through to opt out.

"I don't suppose you can tell us who else is a member," I ask.

She shakes her head, looking genuinely scared. "I can't tell you any more. Please don't ask me."

"Thank you." I reach out to rub her upper arm. "I appreciate you talking to us. It's been helpful."

"Some of the elders are scary and powerful witches," Leah says. "I hope nothing has happened to that woman."

"Me, too," I reply, although I'm more convinced than ever that she's met a grisly end.

Chapter Eight

Arthur and I make pizza for dinner—one of his favourite meals, with barbecue sauce and extra pepperoni—and we sit up at the kitchen table to eat. When I was on my own, I usually ate in the living room, watching TV, but there's something nice about eating properly, with nothing to distract us from each other.

We talk about Jim Small, and what Leah told us, and decide that tomorrow we'll do a bit more digging into Charlotte's life.

"I'm sorry if I upset you earlier," I say.

He looks puzzled. "When?"

"When I said it was no wonder that Charlotte had an affair. I wasn't implying that I think it was excusable. I just really disliked the man."

"I know." He takes a bite of pizza, his eyes on mine. "I'm a bit sensitive to it, that's all, with the whole Lancelot myth."

"I thought that might be the case." I have a sip of wine. "So you never had a friend called Lancelot?"

I don't ask him questions about his past much because it's clear he doesn't like talking about it. It makes him uncomfortable to think of how much time has elapsed since the days when he led an army of warriors against the invading Saxons.

"No. Taliesin was the closest thing I had to a confidante." He glances down at Merlin—the bard's present incarnation—who sneezes. "He might have had a crush on you, but he'd never have acted on it."

I chuckle as I look at the soppy Labradoodle with his shaggy hair and big brown eyes. "Poor Taliesin. Such a ladies' man, and now you don't get to romance anyone!"

Arthur snorts. "Where do you think he disappears to sometimes? He's got a girl in every suburb."

That makes me laugh. I push my plate away and have another big mouthful of wine, building up my courage.

"I want to talk to you about us," I say.

He finishes chewing and leans back in his chair. His blue eyes consider me, cautious, guarded. "Okay."

"I've been thinking about what you said, about it not being the right time for us to… you know… further our relationship." My face heats a little, but I'm determined to see this through. "You said it might be due to Charlotte Small. I keep thinking about that. What do you think she was trying to do? Send you back to the sixth century?"

He frowns. "I don't know. I don't think so." He leans forward then and places a hand over mine. "Don't worry about it."

"You know I can't do that," I reply. "I… I know I said in the beginning that I needed more time, but we've got to know each other better since then. I can't wait forever—I don't want to wait forever." How can I explain how much I love him? How much I want to be with him?

He gets up then, still holding my hand, comes around to my side of the table, and pulls me to my feet. Then he turns me and backs me up against the kitchen worktop. He moves closer, lifting his hands to cup my face. My pulse quickens, and when I look up, all the breath leaves my body at the desire in his eyes.

"I'm crazy about you," he says simply. "And it's not going to be long now until we can be together." He brushes my cheeks with his thumbs. "We have the rest of our lives, Gwen. To explore each other. To get to know each other properly. I want you, I need you, but I'm determined not to rush this. I've waited this long; I can wait a little bit more until the time is right."

Frustration knots my stomach; I still don't understand. But he lowers his lips and kisses me, and I sigh and clutch at his sweater, willing to wait if he continues to do this.

On his palette of kisses, this is a warm orange, luscious and sweet, sending tingles down to my toes, to the tips of my fingers, and the roots of my hair. He takes his time, making it clear that he's in no rush, tilting his head to the side to slant his mouth across mine, and moving his arms around me so he can tighten them and crush me to him.

Oh… he's good at this, and for a moment everything fades away and there's just me and him, the world spinning around us, a blur of colours and shapes. Green grass, tall trees, the blue of the sky, the grey of the stones behind us, the smell of leather and the ash from the fire, the soft whinny of horses, and men talking in low voices.

Then Arthur lifts his head, and I'm back in the kitchen, the sun setting outside the window, flooding the garden with ruby red wine.

"What?" he asks, amused at what must be a startled look on my face.

"I had a vision," I whisper.

His smile fades. "Of what?"

"I think it was of the two of us, back in the sixth century."

His lips slowly curve up again. "Really?"

"I think so. We were outside a stone building, in a camp, I think. I could hear men and horses and smell the fire… You were wearing leather, and you were kissing me, just like you did here."

"I did kiss you a lot," he admits. "So it's not outside the realms of possibility."

I look up into his eyes, filled with wonder. "It's the first time I've remembered my past life. Do you think that's what it was?"

"Maybe." He kisses my nose. "It's nice to think so."

"I really was Guinevere?"

"Yes, sweetheart."

"I didn't believe it," I whisper. "I really was married to you?"

"You were."

"You loved me."

"I did. I still do."

"You really did wait over fifteen hundred years for me?"

He smiles. "I'd wait a million years if I had to. You're worth it."

Tears sting my eyes and tip over my lashes.

"Aw," he says, and he pulls me into his arms. I bury my face in his sweater, thinking about the leather armour he was wearing. "I told you, I'm crazy about you," he murmurs, kissing the top of my head. "I love everything about you. Your fiery hair. The way you sing while you're baking. How you brush Merlin at night, with such gentle hands. The look on your face when you kiss me."

I wipe away my tears. "I'm still frightened you're going to vanish one day. I'm worried that Charlotte has somehow found a way to take you from me."

"I'm not going anywhere," he says fiercely. "You're stuck with me, for better or for worse."

His words echo the marriage vows that people take nowadays. I wonder what we said to each other back then, in the sixth century? I know that Christianity had come to the British Isles by Arthur's time, but he told me previously that although he knew of the Christian stories, his faith was guided by nature, following the cycle of the seasons, the Goddess and her consorts, the Oak and Holly kings. *We left the rest to the monks and the druids*, he told me. So maybe when we married it was more like a handfasting—a pagan commitment ceremony.

Will he want to marry me this time? I'm too shy to ask. Maybe he'll want us to live together for a couple of years first.

I'm getting ahead of myself, though. One thing at a time, Gwen. I sigh and turn to stack the dishwasher, and when we've cleared away, we refill our wine glasses and take them through into the living room.

Some evenings we read, occasionally we play a game. Tonight, we both fancy a movie.

"Choose an old one," he says, so, knowing he likes magical tales, I put on *A Matter of Life and Death*, and we settle down to watch David Niven fight to stay on earth with the woman he loves.

We're about halfway through, cuddled up on the sofa, kissing occasionally, when my mobile rings on the coffee table. Beatrix sometimes calls in the evening, so I pause the movie and pick it up, but I'm surprised to see Imogen's name on the screen.

"Hello?" I answer.

"It's me," Imogen says. "Sorry to interrupt."

"It's okay, we're only watching a movie. What's up?"

"I have some news and thought I should let you know," she says. "Jim Small has been found dead."

I swing my feet around and sit up, startled. "What?" Arthur frowns at me, and I repeat Imogen's words to him. He looks as surprised as I feel.

"His sister went around to his house and found him dead in the chair," Imogen says. "Apparently he died around five o'clock."

I cover my mouth with my hand for a moment. Then I tell her, "Arthur and I left his house at three p.m."

"You were there?" Her voice is sharp.

I swallow hard. "We called in to try and find out more about Charlotte. We talked to him for a bit. He was sitting in his chair watching TV when we left."

"But he was alive, obviously."

"Yes, although he didn't look well. He made us both a coffee, but by the time we left he was onto beer. How did he die?"

"We're not sure yet. When you say he didn't look well…"

"He was sleepy, and his speech was slurred. His eyes were unfocussed, although I put that down to the alcohol. His skin looked… I don't know, greyish. We just crept out and left him."

"Did you find anything out about Charlotte?"

"As you said, Jim suspected she was having an affair. He said she'd disappeared before, so he assumed she'd just gone off with the guy. He said that back in March she started acting differently, wearing nicer clothes and perfume. She became very secretive. She was into astrology, and we found sheets of figures in her study. She was trying to work something out—something to do with Arthur, I think. We also found her sketch books. The latest one contained drawings of three different sites. I'm going to try to work out where they are." I'm waffling a bit. "Sorry, I don't know if that helps with Jim's death."

"It's okay. I have a feeling Charlotte's disappearance and his death are tied together, don't you?" She sighs. "Well, tomorrow I'll officially open a case for her. We need to find her now, firstly to make sure she's safe, and secondly to find out what happened to her husband."

"Can I help at all?"

"By all means, continue to do what you're doing," she says. "Just keep me in the loop, okay?"

"All right," I reply.

"Well, go back to your movie," she says. "And sorry to interrupt."

"Goodnight, Immi."

"'Night, Gwen."

I finish the call and curl back up on the sofa.

"Are you okay?" Arthur asks gently.

"I didn't like him," I say in a small voice, "but I am sorry he's dead." I rub my nose. "I can't believe we only saw him this afternoon. I knew he was unwell. I should have rung someone, made an effort…"

"You weren't to know." Arthur takes my hand. "I thought it was just the beer, too." His kisses my forehead. "Shall we finish the movie?"

"If you like." I press play and settle back in his arms.

I find it difficult to concentrate, though. I keep thinking about Jim Small, sitting in that chair, with his grey skin and unfocussed eyes. How did he die? Maybe he had a heart attack.

It's only then that I remember Charlotte's words from my vision. *I've been in chains for so long, but the two of us are nearly free.*

I shiver. Did Charlotte have something to do with his death? How, if she was already dead?

Chapter Nine

The next afternoon, when Arthur and I have finished work, we head over to Anita Finley's house, Merlin in the back of the car.

Jim had said that Anita and Charlotte had been best friends since they were teenagers, but that they stopped seeing each other, implying they'd had a bust up. I'm keen to find out what it was about, if Anita will talk to us.

"Do you think she might be a member of Morgana's Sisters?" Arthur asks. I'm driving today, heading out to Wells, where Anita lives, not far from Charlotte.

"If she is, she might be able to tell us which branch they went to," I reply. "If she'll talk about it. From what Leah implied, members of the coven are sworn to secrecy."

"Aren't most covens like that?"

"Well, I'm sure they're encouraged not to speak openly about their private practices." I signal and turn onto Anita's road. "But Leah suggested she'd been threatened. They might even have pressed her into signing an NDA."

"What's that?"

"Sorry—a non-disclosure agreement. Basically, you promise in writing not to reveal something."

"And that stops people?" Arthur's view of the law is a lot looser than a modern guy's.

"You can be sued if you don't keep to it," I advise. "Litigation and the threat of losing vast sums of money plays a large part in today's society."

"That sucks," he says, another one of his new phrases.

I chuckle. "It does."

"Not everything is better nowadays."

"No. You're very right there." I pull up outside Anita's home, and we get out.

"It's a nice house," I say, waiting for Merlin to jump down. "A bungalow."

"Sorry, a what?"

"Bungalow. Because you 'bung a low' roof on it."

"Really?"

I laugh as I lock the car door. "No. They originated in India. They're usually one-story houses, often detached. In England, there's so little space and so many houses that detached bungalows are very sought-after, and often expensive. Usually they're owned by older people—it's rare for young couples with families to be able to afford them."

We walk slowly up to the garden gate. "Life was a lot simpler in the sixth century," Arthur states. "No mortgages. A man was expected to build his own house and grow his own food."

"It might have been simpler, but it was also harder." I open the gate.

"It's all relative," he replies. "And people aren't any happier today for all their luxuries and easy lives."

That, at least, is true, and I ponder on his words as we walk up the garden path to the front door.

I ring the bell. It only takes a few seconds before someone answers.

It's a teenager, maybe fourteen or fifteen, with long brown hair and rather too much makeup for a girl her age.

"Hello," I say. "Is your mum home, please?"

"No." She looks at Arthur, and her face reddens.

I can tell he's trying not to smile. "Do you know when she'll be home?" he asks gently.

"I don't know," she says. "She's in hospital."

We both stare at her. "Oh dear," I say. "I hope you don't mind me asking—was it planned, or was it an emergency?"

"She was really sick over the weekend," the girl advises. "Dad rang an ambulance on Sunday night." She reaches up a hand to scratch her nose, and it's then that I see it—the tattoo on the inside of her wrist. A black triquetra with the letters M and S.

"Okay," I reply, "we might go and visit her in hospital. Is she in West Mendip?"

"Yes."

"Thank you for your help."

"Sure," she says. Her gaze remains on Arthur as she slowly pushes the door closed.

"Usually it's Merlin who pulls," I tell him as we return to the car. "Clearly you appeal to young women." He gives me a wry look. I grin and gesture to the driver's side. "Can you drive? I want to ring Immi."

"Interesting that Anita's sick." He buckles himself in and starts the engine. "I wonder if it's connected to what happened to Jim Small?"

"We'll have to find out. Off to the hospital we go."

As he drives, I call Imogen on my mobile.

"DCI Hobbs," she states.

"It's me," I advise. "Can you talk?"

"I have a couple of minutes. Everything all right?"

"I've just been to see Charlotte's best friend, Anita Finley, and it turns out she's been taken to hospital. I'm on my way there now, and I wondered if you could clear it for us to talk to her." I know that the staff at the hospital will only let family in to see her.

"Yes, of course. Wow. What happened to her?"

"Her daughter just said she was really sick."

"I'll be very interested to find out more," she says. "I'll ring them now and clear it for you."

"Thanks Immi. Talk later."

We hang up, just as Arthur arrives at the hospital. He finds a parking spot in the car park, and we leave Merlin there this time and head inside.

Imogen's done her work, and a nurse takes us through the small hospital to Anita's ward. It's a large white room with four beds, all filled with women. Anita is in the corner near the window. A man sits by her side, presumably her husband.

"Excuse me," the nurse says to them as she approaches. "These people would like to speak to you, and the police have given clearance." She gives us a stern look. "Ten minutes only, and no causing her any distress."

"Of course," I reply, and she leaves the room.

The man stands. "Can I help? I'm Steve Finley—Annie's husband." He's in his mid-thirties, with ruffled brown hair the same colour as his daughter's, and he looks harassed.

"I'd like to have a word with your wife," I say, looking at Anita, who opens her eyes as she hears her name. Her skin is the same grey colour that Jim's was, and her eyes also look oddly unfocussed.

"What about?" Steve's tone is vaguely hostile, but I understand he must be worried about his wife.

"It's about a case we're working on," Arthur says easily. "Steve, do you fancy a cup of coffee? I'm sure you could do with a break."

Steve looks at his wife, who turns her head away and looks out of the window. Steve shrugs and says, "Sure," and Arthur leads him out of the room, disappearing down the corridor.

Anita's gaze comes back to me. "Who are you?" she whispers.

I walk up to the bed. "My name is Gwen Young. I'm helping the police with an investigation. I was hoping you'd answer some questions for me."

"What sort of investigation?"

I perch on the side of her bed. "I'm afraid to tell you that Jim Small was found dead in his house yesterday afternoon."

Her eyes widen. "Jim? Charlotte's husband?"

"Yes. You know him, obviously."

"Yes, of course. I don't believe it. How did he die?"

"We're not sure yet; we're waiting for the coroner's report." I rest a hand on her arm and will healing energy to pass from me to her. "But let's talk about you. I understand you fell sick on Sunday. Can you tell me what happened?"

She stares at me for a moment, and then gradually relaxes back into the pillow, some of the tension leaving her body. Her brown eyes study me thoughtfully. "You're a witch," she says. "I can feel your energy."

I nod. "And you're a member of Morgana's Sisters." I turn over her hand and reveal her tattoo.

She withdraws it from me. "How do you know about that?"

"I was involved with a couple of members of the Glastonbury branch."

She stares at me for a long time. Then she says murmurs, "You're the one who caught Mary Paxton and Nancy Armstrong."

I nod, not surprised the news has spread to the other branches of the coven. "I helped the police, yes. And now Charlotte has gone missing, and Jim has died. I'm concerned Morgana's Sisters are involved again."

Her chin quivers. "I shouldn't talk to you," she whispers. Her eyes glisten with fear, just like Leah's did.

"I know your coven demands secrecy," I tell her. "But what about the 'And it Harm None' part of the Rede?"

She gives a short, harsh laugh. "Clearly you don't know much about the Sisters."

"I don't. But I'd like to know more."

She swallows hard. "I can't."

"I can't force you to talk," I say, "but I'm convinced something has happened to Charlotte. I need to find her, and I'm sure you can help."

"If I tell you," she replies, "he'll know. He'll know it was me who talked."

"He?"

She looks away.

I nibble my bottom lip. "Let's start with why you're here. What happened on Sunday?"

"I had terrible sickness and diarrhoea," she says. "I felt really unwell. Steve was worried, and in the end, he called 999."

"Do you know what's wrong with you?"

"Yes," she says. "I've been poisoned."

I stare at her. "What?"

"The doctor ran some tests and found ethylene glycol. It's the main component in antifreeze."

"Antifreeze?"

"You know, like you put in the car?"

"Someone gave you antifreeze?"

Her chin wobbles again. "Yes. Apparently, ethylene glycol tastes sweet, so it's easy to slip into someone's drink."

"Do you know who did it?" I murmur, although I already know the answer, because I'm certain she did the same to Jim. I think about the coffee cups, and the sugar in the bowl that he ladled into his cup. I bet she put it in there.

I so nearly drank my coffee. I shiver as I think of the way I went to sip from the mug, then saw Merlin looking at me. Did he know it was poisoned? I'm sure he would have told Arthur, who would have stopped me from drinking. Maybe he just had a feeling something was wrong.

"I think it was Charlotte," Anita says. "I think she put the antifreeze in a bottle of wine she gave me a few weeks ago. I shared a glass with her and then I remember going to the loo, and when I came back, she gave me the rest of the bottle to take home. She must have put the antifreeze in while I was out of the room. I wasn't very keen on it as it was quite sweet, so I put it at the back of the fridge and forgot about it, but a few days ago I'd run out of wine and I thought I'd finish it off."

"What makes you suspect her?"

She doesn't say anything for a long moment, and then she looks away, out of the window.

"Please," I say softly. "Her life may depend on it." I still cling to hope that what I saw was a possible future, not a definite one.

Anita's expression takes on a mutinous, resentful look then. "If she poisoned me, what makes you think I want to save her life?"

"That's a good point. But maybe it's about taking the moral high ground."

She looks across at the door then, possibly checking to make sure her husband isn't coming in. "If I tell you, do you promise not to tell Steve?"

"I promise," I say, because if I don't, I know she won't reveal what she knows.

She gives a long, shaky sigh. "Everyone in Morgana's Sisters knows the legend of King Arthur."

It's so unlike what I expected her to say that my eyebrows rise, and my heart bangs on my ribs.

"For us, Morgana is a symbol of feminine power and what we can achieve if we put our minds to it," Anita says. "But for most initiates, it's just that—a legend. For Charlotte, though, it's much more than that. She's always been fascinated with the story of King Arthur, ever since we were kids. Over the past... I don't know... five or six years, maybe, she became obsessed with the idea that he's the once and future king—that one day he's going to return."

I'm shaking now, frightened as to what this means for Arthur.

"She's really into astrology," Anita says. "She believes it's possible to use it to forecast events. She began trying to determine when Arthur was going to come back. She's been working on it for years. It was about three years ago, I think, that she became convinced she'd calculated the day of his return."

"When was he supposed to return?" I whisper.

"I can't remember the exact date—it was some time in March this year."

I have to fight against a rise of nausea. Arthur did indeed return in March.

"The nearer we got," Anita continues, "the more obsessed she became, going over the figures again and again. She was sure she'd pinpointed the day, but she didn't know where he'd appear, so she started studying the ley lines."

Some people believe that the earth is traversed by lines of energy that intersect at places of power. I've never studied them, but it wouldn't surprise me if that was the case.

"Charlotte believed that ley lines carry within them the history of the land," Anita says. "She visited places she thought were important to the historical Arthur and tried to match the vibrations she heard there to the calculations she'd done. And one day she came to the coven and announced she was close to discovering where Arthur was going to return."

Chapter Ten

I stare in horror at Anita, but she's oblivious to my fear.

"What did the others say?" I whisper.

"They laughed at her." Anita looks a mixture of both smug and pitying, which makes sense considering they were old friends. "Nobody else believed the legends were real. Everyone thought they were just old stories, metaphors, if you like, for the power of women over men. Charlotte clammed up and left."

"When was this?"

"Back in February."

"Did you fall out over it?"

"No," Anita says. "That came later." She sighs and glances at the doorway again. "I was having an affair." Her gaze comes back to me, somewhat challenging. "Are you going to berate me now?"

"It's none of my business," I reply, glad Arthur isn't there, because I know what he'd think of it.

"He's a local politician," Anita says. "I'd been seeing him since Christmas. I was madly in love with him. I didn't go looking for an affair, but I met him in town, and he was super nice to me and really sexy, and it kind of just happened. Now, I'm sure he seduced me because he knew I was in Morgana's Sisters."

My eyebrows rise. "Really?"

"Definitely. He 'guessed'—" and she puts air quotes around the word "—I was a witch. Even though we're supposed to be secret, I was so flattered he was interested that I opened up and told him things I've never told Steve about being a witch and the kind of stuff that happens at the coven."

"You told him about Charlotte," I guess, and she nods.

"I laughingly told him that she thought she'd found when and maybe where Arthur was going to return. He asked me loads of questions, and when I became exasperated with why he was so interested in her, he got cross and walked out. He didn't call me for a while. The next thing I knew, he was seeing Charlotte."

Tears glimmer in her eyes. She obviously had a big crush on the guy, and she feels betrayed and hurt.

"Do you think he only went with Charlotte because of what she found out?" I ask.

Anita nods. "I'm convinced of it. He used us both. And now Charlotte's missing, and I'm frightened in case Julian had something to do with it."

"Julian? That's his name?"

"Yes. Julian Bauer."

"I don't suppose you have a photo of him?"

She shakes her head. "I didn't dare have any on my phone. But he's well known locally; you can Google him."

I rest a hand on hers. "I'm sorry you've been through so much. I hope you feel better soon."

"What do you think has happened to Charlotte?"

I glance at the door as I hear footsteps, and see Arthur and Steve returning to the ward. "I don't know. I'll do my best to find her, and I'll let you know how she is."

"Not sure about the coffee here," Arthur says as they walk up.

"It's instant," I say, pasting on a grin, even though I don't feel like smiling.

His eyes meet mine, and I know he can see how I'm feeling, but he doesn't comment on it. "The nurse said our ten minutes are up," he states.

"Yes, I don't want to tire you out." I rub Anita's arm. "I hope you feel better soon, and thank you for your help."

"You're welcome." She glances up at her husband. I have a feeling she's going to get the third degree as soon as we're gone.

Arthur won't like it, but I can totally understand why she needed to look elsewhere for love.

We walk out of the hospital and back to the car. Arthur offers me the keys, but I shake my head and get out my phone, pulling up a browser as we get inside. Before he's even pulled away, I have a picture of Julian Bauer up on my screen.

I inhale sharply, and Arthur glances at the screen. "Who's that?"

"It's the man from my vision—the one who pushed Charlotte over the cliff."

"Who is he?"

"A local politician. He seduced Anita to get contact with Morgana's Sisters, and then when she told him what Charlotte had figured out, he left her and seduced Charlotte."

"What a rat." Arthur glares at the road ahead. "So what had Charlotte figured out?"

I swallow hard. "By using her astrology and studying ley lines of energy… Apparently she thought she'd worked out when and where you were due to return."

For a while, Arthur doesn't speak. Then eventually, he says, "So this guy used the women to find out about me?"

"It sounds like it." I dial Imogen's number on my phone. "I've just got to tell Immi something quickly."

Arthur goes quiet again, concentrating on the road, and I look out of the window. Imogen answers within a few rings.

"It's me," I tell her.

"How did it go?" she asks.

"Very interesting on several accounts. The first thing I want to tell you, though, is that Anita was poisoned with antifreeze."

"Seriously?"

"Apparently, the chemical in it, ethylene glycol, tastes sweet, and so it's easily slipped into someone's drink. I'm sure I've read that it makes someone look as if they're drunk—slurred speech, blurred vision, that kind of thing, but if left unattended it can easily kill. And I'm certain Charlotte killed her husband using the same method."

"If you're right and Charlotte was killed on Friday the first of May, how could she have killed her husband yesterday?"

"I think she put the antifreeze in the sugar bowl. I bet she didn't take sugar in her coffee, but Jim had several scoops, and he would have had it every day since she put it there. Anita thinks Charlotte put it in a bottle of wine she finished off over the weekend."

"So why did Charlotte poison them both?"

I tell her about Anita's affair with Julian Bauer, and that she's convinced he seduced her to get into Morgana's Sisters. I end with how he then moved onto Charlotte, and that he's definitely the man I saw in my vision.

"So she poisoned both of them to get them out of the way," Imogen says. "That's pretty cold and calculating."

"There's obviously something about this Julian. He seems to have had a hold over both of them."

"Do you think it's magical?" she wants to know.

"Maybe. I don't know much about that kind of thing." It makes me uncomfortable to think about people using magic to control others. In my world, magic has always been used for good. I'd never dream of using it to harm others, but I know not everyone feels the same way.

"Well, it's a murder hunt now," Imogen says. "Someone's dead and someone else is sick because they've been poisoned. Whether Charlotte did it or not, we need to find her and question her. I don't suppose you've had any more ideas where those cliffs were?"

"No, sorry. I'll keep thinking."

"All right. I'd like to bring Bauer in for questioning too, but I don't really have any formal grounds at the moment. If we could work out which cliffs they were, we might be able to find a witness who places them at the scene, then we can pull him in."

"I'll work on it."

"Okay." She sighs. "By the way, Christian wanted me to ask if the two of you fancied a double date again?"

"Yes, of course." The idea pleases me—something nice to think about. "We'd love to."

"Maybe tomorrow night? Christian thought maybe the Turkish restaurant in Wells for something different? I'll make a reservation for seven p.m."

"Great," I say.

"See you then."

I end the call and slip the phone back into my pocket.

Arthur has been silent throughout. Now, he signals left and pulls in at a pub on the side of the road. It's called The King of Camelot, and the corners of his mouth quirk up as he turns off the engine.

It's too early for dinner. But Arthur opens the door, then pauses and looks over at me. "Come on," he says. "Coffee and a cake. We need a break."

I get out, open the passenger door for Merlin, and we follow Arthur over to the pub. The building is old and low, and obviously very old. The doorway bears a Gothic arch with original carvings, and although the doors have been replaced, I feel as if I'm stepping back through time as I go into the low-ceilinged pub, with its dark-oak ceiling beams and whitewashed walls.

Arthur orders us coffee and we choose a couple of pieces of cake from the cabinet before going outside to the beer garden. It's quiet at this time of day. The pub is at the top of a hill, and the garden overlooks the land leading to Glastonbury Tor, miles and miles of patchwork fields lined with high hedges, filled with crops, cows, and sheep. It's a beautiful afternoon, holding a touch of summer, the wind warm as it blows across my arms, because I've left my jacket in the car.

We sit side-by-side, and Merlin lies beneath the table and immediately stretches out and starts snoring.

"He used to snore as a man," Arthur comments. "Funny how that's transferred into his dog form."

I smile, but my heart is heavy. "Are you okay?" I ask him. "I have a feeling I've upset you."

His gaze settles on mine, and there's such tenderness there that my fears melt away.

"Of course not," he murmurs. "It's not you, Gwen. There is some kind of magic at play here; I can feel it, and so can Merlin. It's obviously to do with Charlotte and her scheming, and maybe this Julian fellow you were talking about. She was trying to find me, and who knows what magic she employed to do that? But it's not you. It's never you."

He lifts a hand, cups my cheek, and brushes his thumb across my skin.

"I thought you might be angry about both Anita and Charlotte having an affair," I mumble.

He smiles. "You know me too well. Lack of loyalty does make me angry. But I'm mostly angry at those men who failed to show their women they're loved. There's no excuse for that."

His blue eyes are the colour of the sky behind him, ringed with a darker navy-blue. He shaved this morning, but there's a hint of stubble on his jaw. He smells nice. It might not be dinner time, but I could put him on a cracker and crunch him up.

"You don't think it's a two-way thing?" I ask. "You don't blame the women for looking elsewhere?"

"It always takes two to tango," he says, another of his new favourite sayings. "But when you're happy, you don't have an affair. Women need tending. Any man who doesn't realize that is asking for trouble."

Against my will, a giggle rises inside me. "You make us sound like seedlings."

"Maybe you are. Tiny green seedlings that have the potential to grow into beautiful flowers if given the right amount of attention." He's not laughing—he means every word.

"So how should a man tend to his woman?" I tease.

"Love her," he says simply. "And show her he loves her, as often as he can. Listen to her speak, and pay attention to her words. Give her everything she wants, if it's in his power to grant it. Treat her like a queen." He smiles then.

"How about kisses?" I ask. "Are they on the list?"

He slides his hand to the back of my neck, and his gaze drops to my mouth. "Always. It's important to keep a woman satisfied."

I tingle all over. His gaze comes back to mine, hot, amused.

"How else do you keep a woman satisfied?" I whisper.

"Feed her chocolate," he says, and laughs.

It makes me smile, and then he kisses me, which fills me with warmth. Beneath the table, Merlin sighs, and I feel the warm sun brushing across us, bringing hope and light. A song thrush serenades us from the nearby oak tree. It feels as if the earth is trying to tell us not to worry; that we can combat the darkness hovering at the corner of our vision.

"I love you," Arthur murmurs against my mouth, and he presses kisses over my cheek, my nose, and my closed eyelids, while his arms stay tight around me, keeping me safe.

Chapter Eleven

That morning, I'd put a couple of lovely lamb shanks in the crockpot, and we have them for dinner with roast potatoes, home-grown green beans and carrots from the freezer, and a rich red-wine sauce.

"I'm stuffed," Arthur declares after we finish off with a steamed pudding and ice cream. "You're determined to make me fat."

"Like that's ever going to happen," I scoff. He runs every morning, and he's active most of the day. "It's me who's going to get fat. I find it hard to stay in shape."

"You were too thin during the hard years," he says, a rare glimpse into our past. "And anyway, round is a shape." He chuckles as I glare at him. "Aw." He gets up and comes over to me as I stack the dishwasher. "You need fattening up," he scolds, pulling me toward him and putting his hands on my hips. "It's a sign of contentment."

"I'm content," I protest. It's a half truth. I'm getting there. I'll be happier when the two of us are together in all senses of the word.

But, as usual, Arthur kisses my nose and turns away, and I sigh as we finish clearing up. I have no doubt at all that he loves me and wants to be with me. I just wish that whatever is standing in his way would—as Immi says—rhymes-with-duck off.

I wipe the worktop down, humming as I clean.

"What's that?" Arthur says as he puts the plates away.

"It's an old hymn, 'When a Knight Won His Spurs.'"

"I don't know that."

"Mum used to sing it to me when she put me to bed."

"Sing it for me," he asks.

So I do, all three verses. It's always reminded me of the legend of King Arthur. It describes how knights used to ride into battle with shield and lance, for God and for valour. It says that although the giants and dragons have now gone, we can continue to fight against things like anger and greed using faith, joy, and the truth.

"That's beautiful," Arthur says when I'm done. "And you have such a lovely voice."

"Aw." I push him. "Sweet talker."

He kisses me. "I mean it. Now it's time for a drink, don't you think?"

We pour ourselves a glass of red wine and go into the living room, where Merlin is stretched out in front of the fire after finishing his dinner. "Shall we read for a bit?" I ask Arthur, and he nods, takes a seat on the sofa, and props his feet on the coffee table. He's finished his book on astrology and is now reading about Alfred the Great, continuing to fill in the gaps of history between his own time and the present, and I wait for him to pick up his book. Instead, though, he takes out his phone, which normally means he's researching something.

Leaving him to it, I sit in one of the armchairs, plug my phone into the speaker on the table, and thumb through Spotify on my phone, looking at my favourite albums. I played Arthur some Enya the other day, and he loved her Celtic-style music. So I choose *Legend*, an old Clannad album that contains the tracks used in the *Robin of Sherwood* series my mum used to love. The series is rather dated now, but there's still something magical about it, and I adore Clannad's haunting music.

"I like that," Arthur says, not looking up from his phone, and I smile.

I've been reading some craft books on knitting and crocheting, but I'm not in the mood for them now. Instead, inspired by the music, I collect my Tarot cards and take them out of the box. I shuffle them slowly, thinking about the vision I had of Charlotte and Julian on the cliff edge. I cut the cards, put the lower half on top of the upper half, and turn over the top card.

Some practitioners use reverse cards, which gives double the amount of meanings to the seventy-eight cards. I don't tend to do that as I'm still learning, but as I turn over the card, it slips from my fingers and lands in front of me, upside down.

It's the Ten of Cups. A man, a woman, and two children sit under a rainbow with fields and a house behind them, surrounded by the ten cups. They're all laughing. It's a beautiful card and clearly has a positive meaning the right way up, showing love, harmony, and alignment. But this fell upside down. It means disconnection and struggling relationships. Julian's feelings for Charlotte were not what she thought they were. He was definitely manipulating her.

On impulse, I draw another card. It's the Moon again. I give a short, silent laugh as I study it, looking at the dog and the wolf howling at the moon, the small lake, the standing stones. It's not uncommon to draw the same card several times when it's trying to tell you something. Secrets and lies. What's being hidden from me?

My thumb brushes the card, lingering on the standing stones. And then suddenly I remember Charlotte's words, *Now we've placed all the stones, I think he's going to ask me to marry him*. Stones. Could she have meant standing stones, like the ones at Stonehenge? But her use of the word "placed" makes me think not. Somehow, I can't imagine the two of them dragging huge Sarsen monoliths across the countryside. But the Moon card is definitely trying to tell me something.

I put the cards back into the box and place them to one side. Then I pull the chest toward me containing the Books of Shadows that belonged to the women in my family. I open it up and study the contents. I run my fingers across the tops of them, trying to relax, to let my intuition guide me. Then, seemingly at random, I pull one out.

It's one of my mother's, and has the name Alice Young on the front. I've read it before, and I turn the familiar pages, feeling a little emotional, as I always do when I see her neat, flowing handwriting and drawings coloured in with pencil. My mother was loving and kind, but also a very private person. She told me about my father, but rarely showed emotion about either him or my grandmother. She disliked the fact that her illness impinged on me, and I've wondered sometimes whether she held back her emotion because she didn't want to overload me with her problems.

I flick through the pages, not sure what I'm looking for, just letting my mind wander, half-thinking about the Moon card, and how everything looks different at night, in moonlight. All the colour is bleached from the world, and it becomes a palette of silver, grey, and black, like an old movie. Arthur would have made a great Hollywood actor—he reminds me sometimes of Cary Grant or David Niven, a gentleman, quiet, strong, and polite…

I turn the page, and my fingers tingle. Clannad's moody music fills my head, and the page seems to shimmer. My mother has written a title at the top. It says Calling Stones.

When you're looking for someone or something, she's written, *place a piece of rose quartz at the locations you've seen them or where you've used the object in the past. When you're done, light a candle and say this simple spell.*

Crystal to crystal, light the way, reveal what's lost or gone astray, Goddess link me with the leys, take me, guide me, through the maze.

The crystals will connect with the ley lines and search the memories they hold for your person or object. They will then emit a beam of light that will take you there.

I stare at the book. I must have read this before, but I'd completely forgotten. How did Mum know about ley lines? I don't remember her telling me about them.

"What is it?" Arthur asks.

I look up at him. He's put his book down and is leaning forward, elbows on his knees, hands clasped, watching me. Merlin has sat up, too, and is looking at me intently. The song has changed. I thought I'd only been reading for a minute, but it's obviously been longer than I thought.

"Calling Stones," I say. His eyebrows rise. I read out the page in Mum's book.

When I'm done, he lets out a long, "Ahhh…" and then picks up his wine glass and leans back.

"Those sites in her sketch book," I say. "They must be connected to you. I think she visited them and placed rose quartz there."

"And she placed her last piece on the day she died," he adds.

"I think so. She must have tracked you down, and once Julian Bauer had that information, he no longer needed her."

"So he knows where I am," Arthur says.

I put the book back in the chest, rise from the chair, and walk over to sit next to him. "If he does, why hasn't he contacted you yet?"

"I wonder how accurate the spell is," Arthur muses. "Your Mum mentions a beam of light that guides the person who cast the spell to the lost person. But Julian killed Charlotte. What would happen to the spell after that? Wouldn't it dissipate?"

"It should do." I hadn't thought of that. "Unless he'd come up with a way to extend the beam after her death. Of course, it's possible it's not the same spell at all. Or it's a similar spell, twisted somehow with dark magic to control you."

"That would make sense." Arthur shivers. "It explains why I haven't been feeling myself lately." He looks away, out through the window, into the dark night. Despite my cooking, he's lost a little weight. There are shadows beneath his cheekbones, and his eyes look haunted.

I get up and pull the curtains. "Well, now we know," I say briskly, "we can do something about it. First we need to find out more about Julian Bauer."

"I was just searching on the interweb for him," Arthur says, holding up his phone.

I try not to laugh. "Internet. Or web—the World Wide Web."

"Oh. Sorry. Anyway, it says he's an MP. What's that?"

"Member of Parliament. They represent constituencies—that's what we call electoral areas in the UK."

Arthur nods. "He's thirty-four and single. He was born and raised in Exeter. He has a degree in English history from the University of Exeter, and he was a secondary school teacher of history for ten years. He plays squash and supports Exeter City Football Club. He sounds like an honourable citizen." His lips twist.

"I wonder what connection he has with you," I muse. "Do you think he's a reincarnation of someone you used to know, like me and Merlin?"

"I don't know." Arthur frowns. "Do you think it's possible to break the spell?"

"All spells can be broken." I nibble my bottom lip. "But you know the limit of my skills. I've never dealt with powerful magic like this. I'm not sure how to do it."

"Would Beatrix know?"

I nod slowly. "She might." I pick up my phone and pause the music. "I'll call her."

I dial my aunt's number, while Arthur collects our wine glasses, promises to refill them, and leaves the room. Merlin lies in front of me, and I prop my feet on him.

Beatrix answers in a couple of rings. "Hello?"

"It's me," I reply.

"Hello, sweetheart. How are you?"

"I'm good, thank you. I was wondering if I could pick your brain?"

"Of course. Fire away."

I summarize what we've discovered this evening about Charlotte and the Calling Stones.

"Goodness," Beatrix says. "So he killed her because he got what he wanted."

"Sounds that way. The thing is, I'm sure the location spell she used has done something to Arthur. He's been quiet lately, and feeling… distracted, shall we say, not himself. And now I'm frightened that Julian Bauer knows where he is. Arthur asked me if it's possible to break the spell. I know that all spells can be broken, but I don't know how. I've never had to do anything like this. I've never dealt with dark magic before."

"I'm glad to hear it," Beatrix replies with some amusement. "Well, it's a difficult one. Hexes or curses aren't easily broken. Sometimes meditating can reveal the source—what kind of hex or curse it is, in which case a witch can try to counter it with another spell. Occasionally self-protection spells can ward out the hex, like building a brick wall to keep out intruders. But I'm not sure that what Charlotte has done is a hex or a curse."

"What's the difference?"

"A hex is a physical spell meant to do harm. A curse is more of a wish, I suppose. Anyone can curse someone else. Only a witch can cast a hex."

"So if it isn't a hex, what is it?"

"I'm not sure. Some kind of binding spell, maybe. Casting a protection spell on Arthur will help. Do you know how to do that?"

"I can come up with something," I say. "But that won't actually break the spell she cast?"

"No. The best way to do that would be to destroy the rose quartz."

"You mean the pieces she placed at the sites?"

"Yes. If you think of it like a spider's web that she's caught Arthur in, if you detach the web from the places it's attached to, it will weaken and collapse."

"Okay. So I've got to work out what sites are in her sketch book and go there."

"It would be the surest way to break it."

"Thank you." Mixed emotions churn in my stomach—determination to help Arthur and not let Bauer beat us; relief that at least I have a plan of action now; and fear, also, that I won't be able to work out where the sites are. And even if I do, how will I be able to find a tiny piece of rose quartz? I doubt she'd have left it somewhere obvious; she'd have hidden it.

I say goodbye to Beatrix, promising to keep her informed. Then, realizing Arthur hasn't come back into the room, I go out into the kitchen. There's no light on, but he's there, leaning against the worktop, looking out at the garden. The moonlight streams in, falling across him like a silver bar. I stand in the doorway for a moment, quietly admiring him. In the semi-darkness, his modern clothes less visible, I can see glimpses of the sixth-century warrior in his stubbled jaw, his broad shoulders. He has muscular arms from wielding a heavy broadsword, and large thighs from controlling his horse. No wonder I fell for him back then. He would have looked amazing in early medieval armour.

He looks over his shoulder then, catching me admiring him. I walk up to him, slide my arms around his waist from behind, and rest my cheek on his back.

He places his arms over mine, and we stand there like that for a long while, in the moonlight, sharing our warmth.

Chapter Twelve

I spend an hour or so reading through other Books of Shadows to find a protection spell, and eventually discover it in one of my grandmother's books. Lizzie's loopy handwriting lists possible ingredients for the spell, and I collect as many as I can, bring them into the living room, and place them on a tray with a white candle and a tiny glass spell jar.

"Sit here," I tell Arthur, pointing to the end of the sofa. I sit at the other end, and we turn and face each other, with the tray between us.

"Are you sure about this?" he asks. "You're not going to turn me into a frog or something?"

"I'll do my best not to," I say wryly as I light the candle. I lean forward and pick up my Tarot cards, leaf through them, and take out the King of Swords—the card I associate most with Arthur. I lay it on the tray.

Next, I take a small amount of each herb in turn and place it in the jar. Basil, black pepper, cumin, marjoram, rosemary, coconut, salt—which protects against pretty much anything, and a few dried blueberries, which are supposed to block a psychic attack. The final thing I add is a small piece of clear crystal. Once they're all in the jar, I top it up with spring water blessed under a full moon and screw on the top.

Finally, I shuffle the Tarot deck, cut it, and offer it to Arthur. He chooses a card and turns it over.

It's the Ten of Wands. A man is carrying ten heavy wands through the countryside, heading for home. Arthur is bearing a heavy weight that's dragging him down, holding him back. Charlotte and Julian have chained him to the earth.

I feel slightly sleepy, and I know I'm descending into a trance again.

Before I forget, I pass the jar through the candle flame and say the spell.

"Mother Goddess, candle bright, protect your servant, day and night, herbs of magic, fruit so sweet, this spell of light is now complete."

Those are the words in Lizzie's Book of Shadows. But as my eyelids grow heavy and my voice lowers, more words spill from my mouth.

"Vines of darkness, earthly tomb, fading light, and gathering gloom, moonlight cleanse and sun dispel, nothing break this crystal shell."

There's a sharp crack as the jar breaks and splinters fly across the room. Bright light explodes from the crystal inside and hits Arthur square in the chest. He flies backward, tumbles off the sofa, and ends up on his backside on the floor. For a brief moment, I can see an egg-shaped shell around him like a forcefield. Then it fades, and there's just his astonished face, his wide eyes staring at me.

He glances at Merlin. "He just said, 'At least you're not a frog.'" He looks back at me, and we both burst out laughing.

After we've picked up the glass so Merlin can't tread on it, and we're sitting back on the sofa, I ask Arthur, "So how are you feeling?"

He rubs over his heart. "It stings a bit."

"I'm sorry about that."

"It's okay." He smiles. "You surprised yourself, I think."

"I never thought I was capable of anything like that."

"I keep telling you how powerful you are, but you don't believe me."

"I figured you were just flattering me," I admit. "Because you wanted to kiss me."

He moves closer, puts his arm around me, leans forward, and brushes his lips against mine. "Do I need to flatter you to get you to kiss me?"

"No," I murmur back, and I put my arms around his neck and give in to his demanding kiss.

*

The next day, around two o'clock after we've both finished work, we get stuck into doing research.

We spread out Charlotte's sketch book on the coffee table and begin with the first drawing. "I wonder what made her choose these three sites," I say. "She had calculations for hundreds of places she obviously thought could be connected to you."

"Maybe she went for those closest to her," Arthur replies. "The strongest contenders for the locations of the legends. It's odd that there are only three drawings in this book, when there were blank pages at the end of the previous one. It's as if she started the new book on purpose because she wanted these pages to be separate. She could have intended to do more."

"Perhaps. Although I'm not surprised there are only three. Remember the triquetra tattoo? Three is obviously a sacred number to Morgana's Sisters." I pull the sketch book closer, and we both peer at the drawing.

"There are sixteen thousand churches in England," I tell him, "and a thousand religious houses, so we've got to narrow it down somehow. We'll start with churches in Somerset."

"Okay."

We look for a list online of Somerset churches on Wikipedia. There are forty-four. We click on each one, trying to match the photos to Charlotte's painting. After about thirty minutes, we realize it's not going to work. A lot of the churches look alike. Many of them were originally Norman, built in the eleventh or twelfth century, but nearly all of them have had later additions and show a variety of architecture. With photos taken from varying angles, it's nigh-on impossible to work out which one—if any—is Charlotte's.

"It might not even be in Somerset," Arthur comments.

"Time for a coffee," I reply. We go into the kitchen and make ourselves a latte. Then we return to the living room with our drinks and a couple of my Mind over Matter Muffins, which contain olives and rosemary and a spell to improve concentration.

"I think better with coffee and food," I say, munching on a muffin. "So, what's the next step?"

Arthur gives a bit of his muffin to Merlin. "Maybe we should note down everything in Charlotte's drawing, and do a search using anything unusual we can see."

"All right, let's try that."

So we pore over Charlotte's drawing, and I make notes on every element we can see within it. It's a pretty little church, but there isn't much to make it stand out from the crowd.

And then Arthur taps the page. "What's that?" It's a diamond shape on the outer wall of the tower over the chancel. Charlotte has embellished it with small black leaf shapes.

"I think it's a clock." I narrow my eyes at the sketch. "They call them turret clocks—clocks on places like churches and town halls.

They're not rare, but this one looks quite big, doesn't it? And I think it's old. It must be special, for her to have made a point of drawing it."

Arthur takes my iPad. "Let's start a search."

He looks for "church clock King Arthur Somerset", which doesn't yield anything interesting. Then he replaces Somerset with South England. Also nothing. He spends another ten minutes trying different variations and looking at photos of the churches the search throws up. Still nothing.

He sits back for a long moment. I finish off my muffin, watching him. He's looking at Merlin, and I suspect the two of them are having a silent conversation, which happens occasionally. Eventually, Arthur pulls the iPad toward him again. "Merlin has a hunch," he says, confirming my suspicions. He types in "church clock Guinevere".

At the top of the search list is The Church of St Mary and St Melor in Amesbury.

"That's in Wiltshire," I say. "Not far from Stonehenge."

"Stonehenge?"

"The huge stone circle," I say. "You must have seen it in your day."

"Of course," he says. "I went to several celebrations there."

"Oh." I'm pleasantly surprised. The henge would have been old even to him.

He clicks on the link, and it takes him to another page about its history. There's a photo of the church. It's a slightly different angle from Charlotte's drawing, but there's no doubt about it—it's the same church.

We both inhale and stare at it. "We've found it," I murmur.

As he's holding the iPad and it's at an angle for me, I let him read it while I drink my coffee.

"There used to be a Saxon abbey there," he says. "It was founded in 979, probably on the site of an earlier abbey." He looks away then, out of the window, lost in thought.

I take the iPad from him. The article mentions Sir Thomas Malory. I know he wrote *Le Morte D'Arthur*, reworking the stories about King Arthur and the Knights of the Round Table. "Malory says that Amesbury was the monastery where Guinevere retired when King Arthur died."

He glances up at me, and we exchange a long look.

"I know," Arthur says eventually.

My eyebrows rise. "What do you mean?"

"We went there," he says. "Near the end, before my final battle. You told me that if anything happened to me, you wanted to leave the world and go into a nunnery. You made me go with you to see the place. We had a big argument there. I didn't want you to do it, but you insisted it was your choice. You wanted to stay the night and have dinner with the Abbess, but I rode off and left you. I hated the place." He frowns at the memory.

It's the first time he's ever mentioned us being anything but happy together, and it makes tears prick my eyes. Guinevere must have loved him very much to be so adamant that she didn't want to go on in the world without him.

"I thought you said we weren't Christian," I comment, a little shakily.

"We were both brought up Christian. You so more than me. That doesn't mean we abandoned the old Celtic gods. Things weren't as black and white back then."

I don't particularly want to go to the abbey and remind either of us of unhappy times, but we don't have a choice.

"So you have strong feelings for it," I say. "That explains why Charlotte might have chosen it, at least."

He runs his hand through his hair. "How far away is it?" he asks.

"About an hour, I think. Use Google Maps." I've already shown him how to use the app, so he types in our location and the church's name. "One hour, eight minutes," he says.

"We'll finish our coffee and then we'll get going."

"I'm sorry," he says. "Maybe I shouldn't have told you that. I think I upset you."

"I'm not naïve enough to imagine that we never quarrelled," I reply. "I just don't particularly like thinking of the end… you know. But we should focus on the fact that we might have found the location of the first Calling Stone. Now we have to work out where Charlotte might have put the rose quartz."

"I wonder whether there's a clue in the drawing?" he asks.

We both look at it again, comparing it to the photo of the church on the iPad. Charlotte obviously sat a little to the north of the person taking the photo, but the view is roughly the same. There's the church itself, with the nave, transepts, and central tower, a tree to the right— possibly a yew, as I know they're often found in churchyards—and a lawn to the front, strewn with gravestones. Charlotte has painstakingly sketched in each individual gravestone, including ones at funny angles.

"What's that?" I peer at the photo and enlarge it with two fingers. On the lawn, near the front door of the west end, is a stone cross. It's well-worn. It looks Saxon.

It's also not in Charlotte's drawing.

"Huh," Arthur says. "Do you think they might have moved it there after she did the drawing?"

"It's possible, but her drawing is only dated March, so I doubt it. For some reason she didn't include it in her sketch."

"Maybe it was her way of marking the spot without making it too obvious," he says.

"Maybe. Only one way to find out."

I go upstairs to get changed, pulling on a clean pair of jeans and a sweater. Then I sit on the bed and open my pack of Tarot cards.

I shuffle them, close my eyes for a moment, and draw a card. It's the Ten of Swords. I frown as I study it. A man lies on the ground on his front with ten swords standing upright in his back. It's one of the more negative cards in the deck, and it refers to hitting rock bottom, to severing ties, and goodbyes. I suppose it's reflecting what happened at the abbey back in the sixth century—Arthur and Guinevere arguing, his death and her grief as she went back to the abbey. It makes sense, but it leaves me uneasy, and I head downstairs with an odd sense of foreboding.

*

Before long, Arthur, Merlin, and I are in the car, heading for Amesbury. Arthur takes the opportunity for driving practice, and I settle back, happy to give over the reins, so to speak. We listen to music for a while, and I only turn it down when we're about fifteen minutes from Amesbury.

"You okay?" he asks.

"I don't know. I feel…" I try to think how to express what I'm feeling. "My stomach has butterflies. My skin feels… itchy. I don't know what that means. Maybe I'm just allergic to the wool in my sweater."

Arthur looks at Merlin in the rear-view mirror. "He says the butterflies are a physical reaction of the nerves in the solar plexus prompting the fight-or-flight response. The itchy skin is a psychic reaction."

"To what?"

"He's not sure."

Merlin's right; I can feel the nerves bubbling away. I'm not sure if I'm anxious that we won't find anything, or anxious that we will. It's the closest we've been to tracking down Charlotte, and it's possible that if we find the rose quartz, we might be able to break the spell that we're both sure Arthur's under. If we don't… I don't want to think what might happen.

"I wonder whether Immi's managed to find out anything," I muse. "I think she's putting a couple of officers on Julian Bauer, to see what he's up to. But she won't be able to bring him in until she has more evidence that he's involved in this."

"Maybe we'll uncover something that will help," Arthur suggests. He reaches out a hand and places it over mine.

I splay my fingers so they interlink with his, and he closes his hand around mine. The A303 is busy but the traffic is moving, so we continue to hold hands while he doesn't need to change gear.

Enjoying his touch, I look out of the window. We've passed through the odd Wiltshire village, but the countryside mainly consists of fields and gently rolling hills. Occasionally, barrows or burial mounds are visible on the horizon, curving above the skyline.

"When were they built?" Arthur asks, gesturing at one.

"Some are Neolithic," I reply, "maybe 3000BC. Others are Bronze Age, up to around 1800BC. It's a very old landscape."

On our left, the ancient site of Stonehenge nestles amongst all the barrows. "You can't touch the stones anymore," I advise Arthur. "You used to be able to when I was a child, but they've roped them off now."

"It makes sense, but it's sad," Arthur says. "I'm sure the people who built it would be disappointed." He peers at the stones. "It must have taken a long time to build."

"We now know there are several phases. A line of posts has been found dating to around 8000BC, so people came here a long time before the stone circle was built in around 2600BC. Amesbury is actually the oldest continually occupied settlement in the UK."

"There seem to be less stones than there were in my day," he observes.

"There were originally eighty bluestones," I reply, "brought 150 miles from Pembrokeshire in Wales. We can only find forty-three today. The sarsen stones were a little later. They make the trilithons—the two vertical stones with the third stone or lintel across the top."

It makes me think of the Moon Tarot card again, with its standing stones. I've been to Stonehenge many times, studied it at university, and read about it in many books. It's always fascinated me, and I've often wondered about its purpose—whether it was purely an astronomical clock to mark the cycle of the seasons, a religious site where people went to honour the gods and goddesses of nature, or whether it was a gathering place where people celebrated the lives and deaths of their ancestors with dancing and feasting.

But I've never felt quite like I do today. I feel as if my whole body is humming like a tuning fork, vibrating with the energy that the stones are emitting. If there are such things as ley lines of energy running through the earth, they will almost certainly cross at places of power like Stonehenge.

This land is so ancient... thousands of years... hundreds of thousands of people... so many have lived and died, giving their energy back to the earth. The sun rises and sets, the constellations pass across the sky. The wheel of time turns again and again... So many hands planting seeds, growing crops, harvesting, blessing the bread, eating it... The cycle of life. So incredibly amazing. So eternal.

"Gwen!"

I snap out of the trance and blink as I realize that Arthur has stopped the car and turned off the engine. We're in Amesbury, sitting right outside the Church of St Mary and St Melor.

Arthur is looking at me with concern, and so is Merlin, his chin resting on my seat as he looks up at me with his big brown eyes.

"I'm all right," I say. "I'm sorry. I zoned out again. Something to do with Stonehenge. I could... feel its power. I think I'm going crazy. Bats in the belfry, as Mum used to say."

"If you do have them, they're very smart bats," he replies. "Come on. Let's investigate the church."

Chapter Thirteen

We get out of the car, and I open the passenger door to let Merlin out. As he jumps down and I close the door, I frown. I can hear a low humming, and it seems to vibrate right up through my feet and leg bones, up my spine, all the way to my skull.

"Weird," I say. I collect Charlotte's sketch book, tuck it under my arm, and walk around the car. "I can feel—" I stop abruptly. Arthur is standing by the driver's door, and he's white as a sheet. "What's the matter?" I ask.

"I feel nauseous," he says. "It started on the way here, but I thought it was car sickness." He breathes deeply, and I can see he's shaking.

"Maybe you need some fresh air." I walk forward, turn, and hold out my hand. "Come on."

He slides his hand into mine, but when I go to walk again, he doesn't move with me. I turn back.

"I can't move," he whispers. Releasing my hand, he massages his forehead. "I have the most awful headache…"

"It must be the Calling Stone." I fight against a wave of panic and open the passenger door. "Sit down."

He lowers himself onto the seat, facing outward, his elbows on his knees, and hangs his head. "Merlin says it's the energy here," he murmurs. "It would have been powerful anyway, but Charlotte's done something to it. It's pooling around the crystal."

"I need to find it and destroy it," I say firmly.

"I want to help," he states. "But I don't think I can."

"Stay here," I instruct. "I'll see if I can find it first."

Arthur mumbles something, but I'm already walking away. I glance at Merlin, who's trotting beside me. "You can stay with him if you like," I suggest, but he just moves closer to me and continues to walk at my side. He obviously thinks I might need him.

I'm trembling a little, both from fear at Arthur's reaction and the power that I can definitely feel running through the earth, but I lift my chin and stride toward the church, determined that Charlotte isn't going to beat us. A gravel path runs through the churchyard, following the line of the church to the front door. I walk down it and then turn right so I'm looking at the church. I know that the majority of churches are orientated east-west, so I'm standing on the west side, facing the nave.

Just in front of the nave, to the right, stands the stone cross.

I open Charlotte's sketch book and lift it so her drawing and the church are side-by-side. She's done a good job; she's captured the beauty of the building, its simple design.

But there's no cross in her sketch.

My pulse quickening, I walk toward it, my shoes crunching on the gravel.

After a few paces, I stop and glance at Merlin. It's oddly difficult to walk. It's like wading through treacle. Merlin shakes himself, then lifts a paw and stretches it out, almost as if he's testing an invisible barrier. He walks forward a few steps like a horse doing dressage, picking up his paws. He can obviously feel it, too.

I press on, conscious of how strange we must look, like two travellers at the Arctic, battling thick, fresh snow, even though it's a beautiful sunny day. Luckily, there's nobody around.

I glance over my shoulder to check behind me and see with some alarm that Arthur has left the confines of the car and is coming after us. "Go back," I call.

He shakes his head and reaches out his arms, for all the world as if he's pulling himself along on a rope. "I can't let you do this alone," he says through gritted teeth as he nears us.

There's no point in arguing with him. I reach out a hand and take his, and then we turn and begin heading toward the cross again.

Goddess, I've never known anything like this. I presume that not everyone can feel it, otherwise I'm sure I would have seen it all over the news. It must be because it's focused on Arthur, and I'm conscious of it because I'm so connected to him.

The air is thick and it's hard to breathe. I feel like I'm pushing my way through a dense fog that's threatening to suffocate me. Arthur's breath is harsh beside me, so I know he feels it too. Merlin's panting, his tongue lolling out of his mouth.

We're not far now, only ten feet or so from the cross. Sweat runs down Arthur's face, and I can feel it trickling between my breasts. His hand is crushing mine.

"Nearly there," I say, pushing the words between my teeth as if I'm pushing pieces of apple through a tennis racket. "Nearly there…"

"I can't." Arthur falls to his knees and retches. The sunlight slants across him, and my gaze blurs, shifts. I blink. Wrapped around Arthur like Marley's chains from A Christmas Carol are layers of thick black vine-like tendrils leading down into the earth. The tips are probing at the crystal shell I created around him, but they're unable to penetrate it. I blink again and they're gone. They're magical; somehow for a moment I saw into the astral plane.

Cold filters through me despite the warm weather. No wonder he's been feeling so strange lately.

Leaving him on the ground, I force my feet forward until I reach the cross.

The top, left, and right portions of the cross are the same size, around twelve inches long; the bottom part forms the post and is about four feet high. The post is engraved with spirals, and the top of the cross with figures that are weather worn and hard to make out.

Not touching it for a moment, I walk around it. I can't see anywhere obvious that Charlotte might have placed the crystal. But then I knew it wouldn't be out in the open. She wouldn't have risked anyone finding it.

I return to the front and bend to investigate the grass. I part the strands with my fingers, searching for any sign that it's been disturbed.

And then I find it. A small square, neatly cut as if with a trowel. The turf lifts easily. Beneath it lies a tiny piece of rose quartz.

Merlin bends his head to look at it, then moves back as if he's been stung and sneezes. I frown and lower my hand over it. He's right; it's hot, and I know if I touch it, it'll burn me.

I glance at Arthur, who's on his hands and knees now, his fingers clutching at the grass. His skin is grey, and he looks haggard. I've got to do something before the black vines tear down the crystal shell.

Using the corner of Charlotte's sketch book, I try to flick the piece of quartz out of the grass. But as the cardboard cover touches the crystal, it catches light. I curse, throw it onto the grass, and stomp on it until it goes out. I need something non-flammable.

Lifting my hands to my hair, I search for the comb I put in this morning. It's a replica of a prehistoric bone comb, one of my favourite possessions that my mother bought me for my twenty-first birthday. I slide it out and lower it to the crystal. It's made of thick plastic. It doesn't catch light, but the tips of the prongs melt immediately as they touch the quartz, and I remove it quickly.

I'm equal parts frustrated and frightened now. How am I going to be able to destroy the crystal if I can't even touch it? I get to my feet and look around. There must be something here that can help me…

I sway a little, unsteady on my feet. The sun is high overhead, hot and unrelenting. I lift a hand to shade my eyes.

The air shimmers.

There's a subtle shift, in light, in temperature.

I blink. It's raining. A grey, typically English day. I look down at myself and see to my surprise that my outfit has changed. I'm no longer in a T-shirt, jeans, and Converses. Now I'm wearing a long black woollen dress over the top of a white linen shift, with a belt around my waist. Folds of white linen hang around my face, and when I lift a hand, I discover that the veil is held there by a slender circlet.

Beside me stands a man, a little taller than I, with greying hair that's braided at the side and held back with a silver clasp. I've seen him before, at the site where Arthur buried his urn of coins. It's the bard, Taliesin, who now exists inside Merlin the Labradoodle. He looks distraught, his face ravaged with grief.

"Lady," he says. "Are you sure about this?" He doesn't speak English—at least, not the English I know—the words sound Celtic, but somehow I can understand him.

I turn my head and look at the building. Except it's no longer the stone church of St Mary and St Melor. About a dozen wooden buildings occupy the site, a central larger one dominating the rest. A wooden cross sits on the top—it's a church. A couple of women are walking across the grass from it to the other buildings, dressed the same as I am. It's an abbey, an old one. I think it predates the later one built in AD979.

I'm Guinevere, come to see out the rest of my days after the death of my husband.

In front of me stands the Saxon stone cross, only now its lines are clean, the figures at the top easily visible.

"I will be fine," Guinevere reassures the man next to me. "I do not want to stay in the world without him, Taliesin. And I feel called to be here. I cannot explain why."

"He will come back for you," he says.

"Then he will know where to find me." She lifts a hand toward the stone cross.

In the present day, I do the same. Our hands rest on the same part of the stone, right in the centre of the cross.

At that moment, she and I are one. I no longer doubt Arthur when he insists I am the reincarnation of his wife. I know it to be so. I remember this moment clearly. My veil is soaked and hangs heavy about my face with rain. Sorrow is a giant rock in my stomach, weighing me down. Arthur is gone, and although Morgana promises me his soul lives on and he will return, I know it will not be in my lifetime. I've lost him, and I wish to spend the rest of my days in solitude and in prayer, doing what I can for the poor and those who need help.

Time shifts, its tissue-paper layers lying over each other, so thin I can see through them from the present to the past.

My love for Arthur has lasted for fifteen hundred years. This man is my soulmate, my husband, my whole life. I love him with every inch of my being, and I can't imagine life without him.

Our love has become part of the earth, our memories flowing through the ley lines, powerful and bright. Charlotte felt it, locked into it, despoiled it. Anger flares within me, supernova bright. It shoots through my veins, red-hot and powerful, as if I've downed a whole bottle of whisky in one go. It travels at great speed down my arms and into the palms of my hands.

It bursts from me like lightning, illuminating the grey sixth-century afternoon and the twenty-first-century day with a glare so bright I can't look at it. At my feet, the rose quartz glows, flares like a piece of sodium thrown into water, and breaks with a deafening crack, despite it only being the size of a pound coin.

Energy hits me in the solar plexus as if someone's swung a baseball bat at me, thrusting all the air from my lungs and throwing me backward about twenty feet. I let out a loud squeal and land on the grass just inches from a gravestone.

And then everything goes black.

Chapter Fourteen

"Gwen!"

I blink. It's Arthur, holding my face between his hands. His face is filled with fear. As I come to my senses, relief replaces the fear, and he bends and kisses me—my mouth, my cheeks, my nose, my forehead, back to my mouth.

"I thought I'd lost you," he whispers furiously, still kissing me. "I thought I'd lost you again."

"I'm here." I sigh as his lips find mine for a longer, more sensual kiss.

When he eventually moves back, I don't know if my dizziness is from being blasted across the lawn or from the kiss.

"Are you okay?" I ask him.

He laughs. "Am *I* okay? You're the one who was thrown across the churchyard."

"I know, but how do you feel?"

He smiles. "The crystal's gone, and so has the nausea. You did it."

"I saw her," I say.

"Who?"

"Guinevere. She did come here, Arthur, when you died. She didn't want to carry on living her normal life without you."

His jaw drops. "You saw her?"

"I *was* her. It was as if I was in two places at once." I struggle to sit up, and he helps me. "This place wasn't here yet," I continue, gesturing at the stone church. "There was a wooden church, and several other wooden buildings. It was the old abbey—the one that predates the late Saxon one."

Arthur sits on the grass beside me. "So she definitely came here after I died."

"Yes. Taliesin was there, too." I reach out and ruffle the dog's fur. "Did he not tell you?"

"I haven't been hearing him well lately," Arthur reveals. "I've felt very… muted. Less sharp. I can hear him now, though." He looks at the Labradoodle and listens for a moment. His expression softens. "He says it was the hardest thing he ever had to do, leaving you here. You were so sad. He says your grief was a deep well, and he knew you couldn't climb out of it. He understood why you needed to withdraw from the world. But it broke his heart to watch you walk into the abbey."

"Aw." I stroke Merlin, who rolls over and puts his feet in the air. "He looks like he feels better now, though."

"Like me, he's been waiting for you to return. He's as happy as a pig in… well, you know."

I laugh. "Come on. Let's get going."

Arthur rises and pulls me to my feet. I go back over to the Saxon cross and run my fingers tenderly across its surface. It's so strange to think that Guinevere was here, touching it in exactly the same place. Already, the memory of being her is fading, but I'll never forget how it felt at the moment that the two of us became one.

I turn away from the church. Arthur and Merlin are waiting. I fall into step beside them, and we head back to the car.

We're nearly there when I stop and look over my shoulder again.

"What is it?" Arthur asks. "Another vision?"

"No. I felt like we were being followed." It's difficult to explain that sixth sense you get when you're certain someone's watching you. My skin prickles, and the hair stands up on the back of my neck. I scan the churchyard and peer at the church, but the only people I can see are an elderly couple slowly making their way toward the west end door.

"Never mind." I open the passenger door and get in. It was almost certainly my imagination.

*

"So you believe him now?" Imogen asks.

The four of us—me, Arthur, Immi, and Christian—are at a Turkish restaurant in Wells, a cathedral city about fifteen minutes away from Glastonbury.

We've finished our starter of hot Turkish bread with hummus, tzatziki, shakshuka, and feta dips, and the waiter has just delivered a huge platter of lamb and chicken shish kebabs with a big bowl of chopped salad, along with more Turkish bread.

Arthur and I have been relating what happened at the church in Amesbury. I help myself to salad and say to Imogen, "What do you mean?"

"You believe you were Guinevere now?"

I glance at Christian, a little embarrassed to admit it in the cold light of day. But Christian has been open-minded enough to go along with everything we've told him about Arthur so far, so I nod and say, "Definitely. At that moment, she and I were one person. I remembered it all. I don't know how."

"You mentioned layers of time." Christian piles the tzatziki yoghurt and cucumber dip on his kebabs. "I think that's an interesting way to look at it—as if time is like an archaeological dig, and you can peel back the layers to see those lying beneath. If we accept that reincarnation is possible, I would think it's unusual for both incarnations of the same person to inhabit exactly the same place. Maybe when that happens, that's when we get déjà vu. And in your case, with Charlotte's spell, and with Amesbury being such a focus of prehistoric power, everything converged to link you together with your past life."

"I love you," Imogen says. We all stop and stare at her. She flushes completely scarlet. "Oh, did I say that out loud?"

I giggle, and Arthur grins. Christian leans toward her and kisses her on the mouth. "I love you, too," he says softly.

"I just meant because you're so open-minded and understanding," she murmurs. She glares at me. "Stop giggling."

"Imogen and Christian, sitting in a tree, K-I-S-S-I—"

"Oh shut up," she replies good-naturedly, and we all laugh.

"So what's next?" Christian asks.

"We try to work out the second site that Charlotte sketched." I tuck into the lamb kebabs. "Wow, these are amazing."

"Try them with the feta dip," Imogen suggests. "So, any idea where the next site is?"

"I've been thinking about that." Arthur pokes at the salad. He's not keen on what he calls 'bits of the garden'. "I think it might be South Cadbury."

My eyebrows rise. "Seriously?"

"What's at South Cadbury?" Imogen asks.

"It's a Bronze and Iron Age hillfort," I reply. "It was also used by the Romans, and again from the late fifth century to the late sixth."

"Arthurian Britain," Imogen says. I was very touched when I discovered that she's been reading up on Dark Age history over the past few months so she can understand more about Arthur and Guinevere's life back then.

I look at Arthur. "I know it's another of the suggested sites of Camelot. Was it a place we ever went to?"

"It was our home," he says.

We all stare at him. I'm conscious of my mouth gaping like a fish's. "What?"

His lips curve up as he chews a mouthful of kebab. "We moved around a lot. The king lived on the coast of what's now Cornwall and we visited him about once a month. We also patrolled the borders. But South Cadbury marked the eastern frontier of his land, and we had a castle built there. An impressive one, if I say so myself."

I knew a hall had been excavated there, and that archaeological finds had placed it to around Arthur's time. But I'd had no idea I'd lived there with him.

"I don't know what to say." My voice is slightly husky. "I feel a little emotional."

"Aw," Imogen says. "That's so lovely. It'll be strange to go back there."

"I wonder if I'll get another vision." I liked seeing back in time, and I'd love to have another glimpse into our past.

"So there was a king of the area," Christian asks, obviously hoping to get some more details from Arthur, who doesn't talk much about the past.

Arthur nods and takes a swig of red wine. "King Conomor of Dumnonia. You know him today as King Mark. I was his Dux—his battle leader, in charge of his army."

Christian has more questions. "Were there raids on his lands by the Saxons?"

"Not in the early days. There was a great battle," Arthur explains, "in which the Saxons were defeated, and there was peace for many years."

"The Battle of Mount Badon," I recall. "Legend says you were there, but it would be too early for you, wouldn't it?"

He nods again. "It happened before I was born."

"But later the Saxons began raiding again?" Christian asks.

Arthur sits back and turns his wine glass in his fingers. "Yes. Under a Saxon king called Cerdic."

"I've heard of him," Christian says. "He was part of a noble British family tasked with manning the old Roman Saxon Shore forts and keeping invaders at bay. But over time, some Saxons settled peaceably and interbred with the Britons, and eventually he agreed to let more Saxons settle in Wessex in return for ruling over them as king."

Arthur's expression shows distaste, which it very rarely does. He doesn't like this man.

"Once he was king," he continues, "the lands he held weren't enough for him, and ambition and greed possessed him. He and his son, Cynric, began raiding Conomor's lands. We clashed several times, and they pushed us back further each time, all the way back to the River Camel."

"The Battle of Camlann," I whisper. It was Arthur's final battle, where he was mortally wounded.

His eyes meet mine. "Yes. I fought my way to the Saxon king. I was convinced that if I could kill him, it would set them back for a while. But Cerdic led a surprise attack. It was his axe that buried itself in me." He rubs his neck, as he often does when thinking about the past.

"Legend has it that he was buried with a ship, to emulate the powerful Saxon kings coming from overseas," Christian says. "But they've never discovered where."

I feel nauseous. It's one thing to learn more about our past lives; it's another to know details about Arthur's death. His soul might not have passed on, but his mortal body died and was buried in Glastonbury Abbey. I still don't understand how he came back. It makes me feel uneasy to be reminded of the tenuousness of his presence here.

"Well he's dead now," Imogen says briskly, "and long gone. Now, who wants more kebabs? If you leave them, I'll eat them all, then I'll be big as a house and I'll squash Christian."

"What a way to go, though," Christian comments. That makes us all laugh, and we help ourselves to more of the food and call for the waiter to refill our glasses.

"Thank you," I say to Imogen a few minutes later, when Arthur excuses himself to visit the Gents'.

"I don't like seeing the two of you sad," she reveals. "Life's far too short for that."

"You're right. We have to make the most of the time we have together."

"About that," she says. "Still no movement on the two of you getting back in the saddle?"

I blush at Christian's smile and sip my wine. "Not yet."

"You need to get your seduction on, girl," she advises. "Want some tips?" Christian snorts, and she grins at him.

"No thank you," I say wryly. "It'll happen when it happens. I was just thinking after what Arthur said here that I think the spell Charlotte cast has had more of an effect than we realized on Arthur. I think it's why he hasn't talked much about the sixth century, and it might also be why our relationship hasn't moved more quickly. I think he's felt mired in the past, and unable to move on. That might change if we can destroy all the Calling Stones."

"You still think there were only three?" Christian asks.

I shrug. "Who knows? It makes sense, with the triquetra being such an important symbol to her." I smile at Arthur as he returns, then ask Imogen, "Any news on Julian Bauer, by the way?"

"I've had a couple of officers start investigating him," she says. "They're looking into where he was on the first of May. He's a busy man. He travels to Number Ten a lot."

"Downing Street," I advise Arthur. "Where the Prime Minister lives." One thing Arthur hasn't shown much interest in at all is politics. I think maybe he had enough of it in his past life.

"He's not a cabinet minister, is he?" Christian queries.

She shakes her head. "Which makes it all the stranger that he's in Downing Street so much. By the way, you'll never guess who he plays squash with?"

I shake my head. "No idea."

"Matthew Hopkins."

My jaw drops. A descendant of the Matthew Hopkins who hunted and murdered hundreds of witches in the seventeenth century, this Matthew is a local journalist currently writing a book on Somerset witches. He knows I'm descended from one of the witches in Glastonbury who was hanged in 1646. I've also discovered that he's a distant relative of the other witch who was hanged back then, a fact he's clearly furious about and wishes to keep secret. I dislike him intensely, particularly because he's developed a twisted attraction to me that he loathes himself for.

"Goodness," I say, and sip my wine. Arthur narrows his eyes at me. Imogen glances at him, then at me. They both know I'm not going to let it rest there, but for now I lower my gaze and finish off my dinner.

"Anyway…" Imogen obviously decides to change the subject. "We should find out some more over the next few days. And we should hear back from the coroner as to how Jim Small died. If it *was* antifreeze, that doesn't look good for Charlotte."

"I would say falling from a cliff onto the rocks looks even worse for her," Christian comments.

"Good point." She pinches the last of his kebab. "Do you mind if I get fat?"

"All the more to hold onto," he advises.

I smile. I'm so pleased for her. She's had her ups and downs relationship-wise, but she really seems to have fallen on her feet with Christian.

Now, if I can only work out how to locate and destroy the other two Calling Stones, I might be able to grab a bit of that happiness for myself…

Chapter Fifteen

On Friday, I spend the morning baking and serving in the café. Delia came up with a few suggestions for new muffins, including one I really liked the look of—lemon chamomile muffins made with chamomile tea. The herb is wonderful for anxiety and relaxation, and Delia's created a spell for anti-anxiety, so we make the muffins and say the spell together, and I design a new label for the cabinet: Relaxabuns, which we both think is really funny.

At two, I make my way to the field unit. Kit Vinson is starting a new dig at Wessex Castle. The castle is actually a nineteenth-century Jacobethan-style country house that's been turned into a hotel. It looks similar to Highclere Castle where *Downton Abbey* was filmed. Recently, though, while digging the foundations for a new set of stables to the east of the castle, the owners discovered evidence of a Saxon settlement, and it needs to be excavated before they can continue. Kit's heading a team that starts work next week, and I'm hoping to be able to help.

Today, we're finishing off the financial planning for the dig, so I'm tied up with paperwork, and by five o'clock, I'm ready for a break. When Arthur turns up, I collect my jacket and handbag, and we wander out into the May sunshine.

"Off to Cadbury Castle," I declare.

He raises an eyebrow. "Are you sure? Don't you want some dinner?"

"We can have it when we get back." I don't follow him when he heads to the car, though.

He turns and raises an eyebrow at me. "What?"

"There's someone I want to see in town first," I advise him.

He tips his head to the side. "Who?" When I don't answer, his smile fades and his brow darkens. "No."

Now it's my turn to raise my eyebrows. "What do you mean, no?"

"We're not going to see Matthew Hopkins."

"You're very welcome to stay here. Merlin and I will go." I turn to set off in the opposite direction.

He catches my hand. "Gwen…"

I turn back. "I want to ask him about Julian Bauer. I'm quite determined, Arthur. You're not going to be able to talk me out of it."

"The man's a maggot," he says.

That makes me laugh. "He is. But he's a maggot with powerful friends. And he did help us solve his sister's murder last time. He turned his girlfriend in when he could easily have kept quiet. He's not entirely evil."

"He's near enough," Arthur mumbles.

"I'm not trying to convince you he's a nice person," I say. "I just want to see if he's willing to tell us anything about Bauer."

"Fair enough. But be aware that he might tell Bauer we've been asking after him."

I hadn't considered that. Hearing that a café owner was chatting about him might not ring any warning bells to Bauer. Discovering that a guy called Arthur was trying to get information from Matthew might.

"Maybe you should stay outside the office," I tell Arthur.

He scowls. "I'm not leaving you alone with him."

"It's broad daylight. I'll take Merlin. I can look after myself," I tell him gently. "I don't always need saving."

His lips curve up. "No, I can see that."

"Why don't you get us both a latte and a roll for the journey?" I suggest. "And I'll meet you at the car?"

"All right." He watches me go, then disappears into the café.

I blow out a breath and look down at Merlin as we turn into the high street. "I hope Matthew behaves," I say to him. "We'll never hear the end of it if Arthur has to come and rescue me."

I know that the office of the local paper is open until five thirty. We head down there, and I open the door, which jangles to announce our arrival. Matthew is sitting at his desk, and he looks up and frowns as Merlin and I go in.

"No dogs," he says.

There's no sign saying as much, so I ignore him. "Good afternoon. How are you, Matthew?" I'm conscious that his sister was murdered last month, and that it was his girlfriend who did the deed. That must have had an effect on him.

"I'm okay," he says. He gets to his feet and comes around the desk to stand in front of me. His gaze slides down me, a little more intimately than I'd like. Thank the Goddess Arthur isn't here, or he'd have punched Matthew for that. "You look good," he says.

"I… um…" My face warms.

Nowadays it's rare for a man to pay a woman a compliment outright. He's flustered me, and he knows it—his eyes gleam with private humour.

He's a good-looking guy, although secretly I think he's past his best. In his late thirties, he's obviously attempting to fight against the aging process. His hairline has receded a little, so he wears his hair short and spiky in a style that's too young for him. His tan doesn't look natural. He works out and plays sport, so his shirt stretches across tight biceps and an impressive chest, but I note that his wrist and ankle are strapped up; he's feeling knocks more than he used to.

I'm conscious that he kissed me a few months ago, against my will, and also that he had Sir Boss—the suit of armour in which Arthur resided—temporarily removed from the Avalon Café. He only finds me attractive because he can't have me. I'm sure there are lots of women who'd be thrilled to have Matthew Hopkins sweep them up and kiss them senseless, but I'm not one of them. He needs to settle down with one woman who'll keep him in check and have a couple of kids to help him grow up, but I can't see it happening anytime soon. As soon as a woman stands up to him, I'm sure he's off out the door.

I move backward so I can perch on the desk behind me and put a bit of space between us. At least today there are a couple of other people in the office—a woman in the room out the back, making coffee, and a young guy doing some photocopying. It makes me feel a bit better.

"I wondered whether you could help me with something," I ask. I don't adopt a flirty tone, but I do smile.

His eyebrows rise. "Oh?"

"Can you tell me anything about the MP, Julian Bauer?"

He studies me. "Why?"

"Because I heard on the grapevine that you were friends with him."

His lips twitch. "I meant why do you want to know, Gwen?"

"I want to write a letter to him about something, and I thought it would help to know a little about him."

He tips his head to the side, considering how to reply. His green eyes—a few shades lighter than mine—are half-lidded and sultry. I think he's attempting to picture me without any clothes on. I try not to shudder.

"What kind of letter?" he asks.

"That's none of your business."

"Something about witchcraft?" He's determined to prove I'm a witch.

"If it was, I'm sure you'd be interested," I say, raising my voice a little, "considering your close connections to the Craft."

He glances over his shoulder, glares at the young lad who's looked over at us, and then his gaze comes back to me. I know he doesn't want anyone to know he's descended from one of the witches hanged here in the seventeenth century. I wish I'd been a fly on the wall when he discovered that. I can only imagine his fury.

"What do you want to know?" His voice holds a touch of bitterness, and I feel a twinge of guilt. What I'm doing could be called blackmail, and that doesn't sit well with me.

Then I remind myself of what I'm sure Bauer has done to Arthur, and lift my chin. "I don't know. I'm just looking for an insight into the kind of person he is."

Matthew shrugs. "What you'd expect an MP to be. Presentable, loyal, and trustworthy on the outside. Ambitious on the inside."

It's a surprisingly honest summary. "Do you like him?"

"Only a woman would ask that," he says, amused. "I play squash with the guy. See him socially sometimes. He has a good sense of humour, plenty of money, and a lot of contacts. We're not bosom buddies. He's not going to tell all his secrets to a journalist."

He moves a little closer to me, and I can't back away because I'm perched on the desk. Merlin growls, but Matthew ignores him, looking down into my eyes. "What's this really about?" he murmurs. "You're playing detective again, aren't you? What are you investigating this time?"

If I tell him anything, there's a chance he'll pick up the phone and tell Bauer all about it. It's a risk, but equally I know it's only a matter of time until Bauer tracks Arthur down. If Matthew can help at all, I have to take the chance. Deep down, even though he's a journalist, I'm convinced he's an honest man. If he turned in his girlfriend, I don't think he'd protect a friend if he suspected they'd done something illegal.

"I'm looking into the death of one of Beatrix's students," I tell him. "Charlotte Small."

"I heard she'd disappeared," he says. "And that her husband died on Tuesday. Are the two connected?"

I glance around. "We suspect she poisoned both her husband and a friend of hers who's in hospital, recovering."

His eyebrows rise. "Oh, interesting. But what's this got to do with Julian Bauer?"

"I think Charlotte was having an affair with him."

He studies me for a long time. "Was?" he asks eventually.

"I think she's dead."

He swears softly. "And you think Julian had something to do with it?"

I don't reply to that. He frowns and looks away, obviously thinking it over.

"Did you ever hear him talk about her?" I ask.

He shakes his head. "He mentioned an Annie once, but when I questioned him about her, he just laughed and refused to say any more."

"I think that might be Anita Finley. She's Charlotte's friend, the one who's in hospital. She's married. They were having an affair, but Bauer left her for Charlotte. Charlotte put the antifreeze she used to poison her in a bottle of wine a few weeks ago, presumably to clear the way for her and Bauer, but Anita didn't drink it until this weekend."

"Wow." Matthew steps back and sits on his desk.

I nibble my bottom lip as I think about whether to tell him the final piece of information. If anything is going to convince him that Bauer is bad news, this is it, but it does mean discussing the one thing that Matthew hates about me. I'm also not sure how much he knows about his sister.

The last thing I want is to be responsible for another Matthew Hopkins witch hunt. Equally, I'm trusting my gut feeling that there's something bigger going on here, and I'd rather have Matthew on my side.

I decide to go for it. "Charlotte and Anita were both members of the coven called Morgana's Sisters," I tell him.

"They're witches?"

"Yes. All members of the coven have a tattoo here." I show him the inside of my wrist. "It's a triquetra, and the letters M and S."

He stares at me. "Valerie had a tattoo like that."

"I know."

"You're saying she was a member of this coven?"

"Yes. She was a member of the Glastonbury branch. Charlotte and Anita are members of the Wells branch."

He narrows his eyes at me. "Why are you telling me this? I know you're a witch. Why would you tell on your friends?"

"They're not my friends. I'm not a member of the coven." I show him my arm, free of tattoos. "But I've spoken to members of it, and I don't like their methods. Whatever you think of it personally, witchcraft is a religion that involves respect for nature and each other, and that's not what they preach."

"So what's Julian got to do with any of this? Are you saying he knows?"

I'm not going to tell him about what's happening to Arthur, or about Charlotte's sketch books. But I don't think there's any harm him knowing that Julian's involved.

"Oh, he knows," I say. "It's why he left Anita for Charlotte, because she had some information he needed."

Matthew studies me for a long time. I stay still, although my heart's banging away inside me. Why am I doing this? He has hardly proved himself to be a good man in the past. Have I said too much? I've not openly admitted anything, but I might as well have. I've confirmed to him that I know about and believe in witchcraft. What if he takes it on himself to hunt down the members of Morgana's Sisters? To pursue and harass innocent women? To harass me even more? How will I feel then?

I wait for him to tell me he's now even more determined to take me down. To tell me I sicken him, and that he wants all witches to die.

Instead, he says, "Julian wears an odd ring."

I swallow hard, feeling slightly dizzy that he's not immediately yelling at me. "What kind of ring?"

"At first I thought it was Masonic—you know, the square and compasses. But when I looked closer, I saw it was like a triangle made from three arcs."

"The triquetra," I whisper.

He nods. "It also had two small symbols coming out of the top. I think they were like..." He hesitates. "Horns."

"The symbol of Herne the Hunter," I tell him. "The Goddess's consort. It could mean he's a warlock. That's like a male witch, but dealing in dark magic."

Matthew's face shows his distaste. "I don't want to know the details. But I will look into him, if you think he's connected with Charlotte Small's disappearance."

"Thank you." An uneasy truce reached, I stand, feeling awkward. "I appreciate your help."

"Don't think that because you're not a member of that coven, it means I'm okay with what you do." He glares at me. "You found my sister when she was murdered, and you helped uncover her killer. But you're still a witch. And I'll never forget that."

There's nothing more to win here. I back away to the door, let myself and Merlin out, and close it behind me.

Chapter Sixteen

I walk back to Arthur, and we get in the car and head off to Cadbury Castle while I tell him about my meeting with Matthew.

"So Bauer is definitely involved somehow," he says. "Do you reckon the ring marks him as part of another coven?"

"It could be a sub-group of Morgana's Sisters—like an elite group. Both Leah and Anita referred to Elders." I shiver. "It makes me very uneasy to think that this is more than petty squabbling between locals."

Arthur looks out of the window, and I leave him to his thoughts as I drive.

It's a pleasant thirty-minute journey through the Somerset countryside to the hillfort. We park at its base in Castle Lane, by an old sign that says "Leading to Camelot Fort", and walk up the lane past banks of nettles flanked by oaks and horse chestnuts. Black-and-white cows peer down at us from the top of the lane, and we have to navigate a stile to reach where the ramparts mark the beginning of the site.

It's a blustery spring day, and heavy clouds mar a blue-grey sky, promising rain in the not-too-distant future.

My heart races as we climb to the top of the fort, and it's not just from the physical exertion. The air has the same heaviness here that it had at the church in Amesbury. I studied Charlotte's drawing earlier, and I'm convinced he was right, and this is definitely the site she sketched. That means dark magic is chaining Arthur to this site, and maybe me as well, indirectly. The memory of those black vines wrapped around him at the churchyard is vivid in my mind. I haven't told him about them, because it was so unpleasant and it wouldn't do him any good to know. But I can't stop thinking about them. I have to free him from them.

We walk up the four terraced ditches and banks to the plateau at the top, Merlin running ahead of us. My stomach flutters with butterflies the same as it did at the church. This time, I know it must be connected to my previous life. I lived here, with Arthur and Taliesin. It's such a strange thought. This place would have been as familiar to me as my mother's house in Glastonbury.

At the top, we stop to look around. There's nobody up here at nearly six p.m. on a Friday evening. There is a 360-degree view of the Somerset countryside in all its glory—brown and green fields outlined with hedges and trees, dotted with the occasional village. I can even see Glastonbury Tor, way off in the distance.

I turn and look across the plateau of the hillfort. It's a huge site. I read a little about it last night. A barricade surrounded the edge, and there's evidence of a forge inside and a Roman temple. But by the sixth century, the main attraction would have been the great hall. They've found post holes that indicated it was one of the largest known settlements of its time. Arthur might not have been a king, but as the head of the king's army he obviously had substantial wealth.

"The hall went from here," Arthur says, indicating the ground ten feet behind us, "all the way to here." He walks halfway across the plateau. "Outside it were smaller houses and barns. But the hall itself was magnificent."

He looks up as if he can see the walls rearing above his head. I try to picture how it might have looked. It would have been made from wood, with intricately carved and painted beams and pillars, and maybe woven tapestries on the wall. Wooden tables would have lined the walls, and a large hearth would have stood in the centre.

Arthur's gaze comes back to me, holding a touch of mischievousness. "We got married here."

My jaw drops. "Really?"

"We danced here for hours." He takes my hand and leads me to what must have been the middle of the hall. The wind tugs at my long skirt and plays with the strands of hair around my face, and I feel a spot of rain on my cheek. Arthur just laughs, turns me into his arms, and proceeds to dance with me, turning me around and around. He seems full of joy, comfortable with his memories.

"The flames in the hearth sent shadows dancing on the walls," he murmurs. "It was before the famine, and there was so much food. We had the best musicians playing all night. And you looked so beautiful in your blue gown."

"Blue?"

"It was the colour of wedding dresses back then. The symbol of purity." He touches my hair. "You wore it down, and it hung past your hips in red waves."

"What did you wear?"

"A very fine dark green tunic. My mother made it for the day."

"Your mother?" It's the first time he's mentioned her.

He turns me around. "Her name was Eigyr—she was Welsh. You know her as Igraine. She loved you. Morgana was there, too, in a dark-red gown. They both looked beautiful, but you outshone everyone else in the hall." I blush, and he smiles.

"Did we exchange rings?"

He lifts my left hand to look at it. "I gave you one. It was gold inlaid with garnets that came all the way from India."

"India!" I'm surprised by the distance it would have travelled, although I know the Mediterranean trade networks stretched far and wide through the Roman ports. The garnets must have cost him a small fortune, though.

"I was very proud of the ring," Arthur says. He looks away, across the hilltop. He's obviously remembering something.

"Was Taliesin there?" I look at Merlin, who's rolling about on his back, snapping at a dandelion.

Arthur's gaze comes back to me and he smiles. "Of course. He sang for us for hours. Then he drank too much and passed out under one of the tables."

Merlin stops wriggling and glares at him, and we both laugh.

"I wish I could remember," I whisper, disappointed that I haven't had a vision.

Arthur stops dancing and pulls me into his arms. "We'll make new memories of our own." He kisses me then, and I sigh and put my arms around his neck, holding him tightly.

I envy the girl I was back then, living in simpler times. But of course, it's easy to say that with hindsight. There would have been no antibiotics, no advanced medicine at all. There was famine and war, and life would always have been lived on a knife-edge. But maybe knowing how fragile it was made it sweeter?

Merlin barks, and we part and look across at him. He's standing by some kind of monument for visitors. It's chest-high and cylinder-shaped. Something occurs to me then. I lower my backpack, take out Charlotte's sketch book, and open it. She must have been standing not far from where I am now when she sketched the view, and she was obviously facing the monument because there's a distinctive oak tree to the right with one long branch that she's sketched.

But there's no monument.

"It's there," I whisper, and I stuff the book back in the pack and cross the plateau.

It's only as we near the monument that I get the first heavy, dragging feeling I felt at the church. Arthur stops walking, and Merlin shakes himself, so I know they're feeling it too.

"It's here," Arthur says.

"I know." I push forward through the invisible barrier. It's not as strong as the one at the church—is that because we've already destroyed one of the Calling Stones? I think of how Arthur has started talking about his past—is that also a sign that the hold Charlotte had on him is weakening?

Encouraged by the thought, I reach out for the monument and haul myself toward it. The brick cylinder is topped by a large circular metal plate. The centre reads "Cadbury Castle A.D. 2000". Radiating out from the centre are arrows that show the direction and distance to various historic places—Stonehenge, thirty-two miles; Avebury, forty-one miles; Tintagel, 108 miles.

There's nowhere for Charlotte to have hidden the crystal on the surface, so I'm guessing it must be in the grass at the base. I drop to my knees and begin parting the grass to find where she removed the turf to bury the quartz.

I shiver, only realizing then that the temperature has dropped. Rain begins to fall on the monument, turning the creamy-coloured bricks a dark brown. I've been an idiot and left my jacket in the car, and droplets soon soak my thin sweater and hair. Determined not to let it stop me, I search through the grass, finding stones, a snail shell, a cigarette stub, an old sweet wrapper.

It's raining harder now. I glance up to see that the sky has turned iron-grey. Gosh, that happened quickly. There's a flash of lightning, and about six seconds later, a boom of thunder rolls across the sky, making me jump.

"That's no ordinary storm," Arthur says.

I stop searching through the grass and look at him. "What do you mean?"

At that moment, there's another flash of lightning, and then this time the thunder follows after a count of two. He's right—the storm is moving much faster than normal, heading our way.

He crawls toward me, although it's obviously difficult for him to do so. My vision blurs, and I see them then—the black vines snaking around him, like long fingers coming out of the ground, trying to pull him into the earth.

Merlin appears beside me, and he sinks his front paws into the grass and begins to dig, reminding me of the reason why I'm here. I should have brought a trowel with me, I think as I claw my fingernails in the earth and scrabble around the base of the monument.

Then Merlin squeals and jumps back, and I move to his side to see he's unearthed the rose quartz, which is glowing brightly in the dim light. That's great—but how do I destroy it? The monument wouldn't have been there in the sixth century, so it's not as if I can touch it in the same place that Guinevere would have done like I did with the cross.

I need to connect with her again, to be her, here, with Arthur, her husband, all those hundreds of years ago when the great hall towered above us…

Following an instinct I didn't even know I had, I get to my feet and wander away from the monument, past Arthur, who's still on his knees, and into the centre of the plateau. The rain hammers down, soaking me, trying to hamper my efforts, and I know it's being guided by someone who's determined to stop me from destroying the second Calling Stone.

But they don't know the depth of my love for Arthur, and how much I want to help him. I lift my face to the rain and embrace it, let the natural energy on this plateau fill me and shine through me. Lightning cracks and thunder booms, but it's just the Goddess speaking to me, and I close my eyes and inhale the sweet fresh air.

And then I open my eyes. I'm in the great hall. The air smells of woodsmoke and cooked meat. The place is alive with colour, from the richly embroidered tapestries on the walls to the painted beams to the jewel-like clothing of the people who are feasting and dancing around me.

And this time, Arthur's there. He stands a few feet away, talking to a woman who looks a little older than he is, with long dark hair—Morgana? He turns and sees me looking at him, laughs, and comes toward me. He's so handsome, his green tunic much more intricately woven than I thought it would be. His dark hair has been braided with silver clasps, which also adorn his thick beard. But the eyes are the same—bright blue and filled with love.

To the right stands another person. I look at them, but I can't make them out. Are they in the sixth century or the twenty-first? Maybe they're in neither. It's as if they're standing in shadow, just a shape—I can't see a face, or even tell if it's a man or a woman. Cold filters through me that has nothing to do with the rain soaking my skin.

The person raises his or her hands, and thunder booms. They're the one controlling the storm.

For a moment, I think I'm going to fail. They're too strong for me. I'm only a glorified cook who bakes muffins that make people happy. Why did I think I could fight someone as powerful as this?

On the rainy, windswept hilltop, Arthur reaches out a hand and takes mine at the same moment that he did in the great hall.

Light flares from us. It increases in brightness until I can't bear to look at it, a tiny supernova, taking my breath away with its brilliance. The rose quartz at the base of the monument screeches like an animal, and then it explodes. A wave of energy sweeps over us, and the sixth century fades like a watercolour painting in the rain, leaving just twenty-first century me, cold, wet, and exhausted, and more than a little afraid of the shadowy figure who so obviously wants us to fail.

Chapter Seventeen

An hour later, we're home, I've had a hot shower, changed into clean, dry clothes, and I'm sitting on the sofa with a hot water bottle and a mug of tea.

"You're taking on too much," Arthur scolds. He places a blanket over me that I don't really need, but I take it anyway, aware that he wants to feel as if he's doing something.

"It's got to be done," I reply mildly. I sip my tea, watching him over the rim as he prowls across the room. Merlin sits by me, his chin on the sofa, looking up at me with soulful eyes. He's worried about me, too.

I haven't told them about the shadowy figure, but I know they can both sense my fear. Arthur stops pacing and observes me for a moment. In my mind's eye I can still see him as he looked back then, on the day of our wedding, bearded and in that beautiful green tunic, laughter in his eyes as he danced with me. Now, he looks sombre and worried. I don't want to see him like that. I want to make him laugh again.

"Merlin saw him," Arthur says, "so you don't need to hide it from me."

I glare at the dog. Merlin glares back at me.

"I don't like that you feel the need to keep things from me," Arthur adds. "I don't need protecting." His look is stern. And a little bit sexy.

"Yes, boss," I reply.

His lips quirk up. "Don't make me laugh when I'm telling you off."

"You're a good dancer," I say. "Light on your feet for a big guy."

He puts his hands on his hips, but he doesn't say anything. His expression has softened, though, and I know he's thinking about our previous life.

"I feel like I have amnesia," I tell him. "It's strange that you're able to remember the time we spent together when I can't."

"Actually, I was thinking about watching you up on the hilltop, in the rain." His gaze caresses my hair. "You looked like the goddess of the weather, standing right in the middle of the storm, soaked to the skin."

"You're only saying that because the rain turned my white sweater transparent."

"Maybe."

We both smile.

"Was it Bauer?" he asks, surprising me.

"Who?"

"The shadowy figure." He sits on the sofa, just down from my feet, lifts them onto his lap, and massages them through my socks. "I know that storm wasn't natural. Do you think he did it?"

I shrug. "We don't know anything about him yet. We don't even know if he has magical powers. But at least we're two Calling Stones down, and only one to go."

"About that." He lifts Charlotte's sketch book from the coffee table. "I think I might know where the last site is."

My eyebrows rise. "Really? Where?"

"It reminded me when I saw it on the monument at South Cadbury. It's quite obvious when you think about it. It's Tintagel."

As soon as he says it, I'm sure he's right. It's the legendary birthplace of King Arthur, where Uther Pendragon killed Gorlois and took his wife, Igraine, as his own. I think of Charlotte falling from the cliffs and realize that could easily be the place I saw in my vision.

"Were you born there?" I ask.

"No, I was born in Wales. But King Conomor lived there, and I spent a good portion of my adult life there, when I wasn't at South Cadbury Castle or out on the road. It's important to me. It makes sense that Charlotte chose it."

I sip my tea. "That's true."

"While you were having a shower, I took a look at Google Maps." Arthur turns on my iPad and shows me. "I marked Amesbury Abbey, South Cadbury Castle, and Tintagel on there. And look."

The three sites form a straight line from east to west.

"It must be significant," he says.

"In Christianity, burials are always aligned east-west," I say slowly. "Altars in churches also nearly always face east, with the main entrance at the west end. It's because Christ's second coming is supposed to be from the east. But even in prehistoric times, burials and monuments were also aligned that way due to the rising and setting of the sun. Whichever way you look at it, the east is seen as the place of return. It must be one reason why she chose those three sites—she must have needed the alignment for the Calling Stones."

Arthur shivers. "I'll be so glad when this is all over."

"Me too." I finish off my tea. "Time to start dinner. And then first thing tomorrow, we'll head off to Tintagel."

*

Later, when I go to bed, I take my Tarot cards with me, and when I'm under the covers and it's all quiet, I shuffle the cards, and cut them. I turn the top card over.

Oddly, once again the card is upside down, even though I don't reverse any of my cards before I shuffle them.

It's the Ten of Pentacles. A boy sits on his grandfather's lap, while his parents talk in the background, by the family home. Two dogs and the boy's sister are in front of him. All the members of the family are dressed affluently, and the right way up, the card depicts wealth and financial security. Upside down, though, it shows the dark side of wealth, or even financial ruin.

The meaning is puzzling, but not as puzzling as the fact that this is the fourth Ten card I've drawn in the past few days. That's got to mean something, but I have no idea what.

I ask for clarification and turn over another card. It's the Wheel—the tenth card of the Major Arcana. Another reference to ten. The picture is like a roulette wheel, with a ball spinning around the outside. The centre is divided into eight drawings of a woman, showing every emotion from pure joy to deep despair. It tells us to enjoy the good times because they don't last, and equally not to worry during bad times because they will pass.

Which does it mean this time?

There's no way of telling, and I turn off the lights and close my eyes, knowing I need a good night's sleep before we head off to Tintagel tomorrow.

I lie awake for a long time, though, staring into the darkness, before sleep finally claims me.

*

On Saturday morning, I text Imogen where we're going to keep her in the loop, and then we set off. I drive, because I'm not convinced that Arthur won't turn the car around at some point and refuse to go there. He's very reluctant to put me through the destruction of another crystal, and I'm equally as determined I'm going to do it.

It takes us nearly two-and-a-half hours to get there. It might have been straight as the crow flies, but the traffic is relatively heavy as people head to Cornwall for the weekend, and the going is slow.

It's nearly midday by the time we arrive. We park in the public car park and get out of the car.

"Wow," Arthur says. "It's changed a lot from when I was here last."

I've been here before, but I'm still amazed at the extent of the site. The sea has eroded a neck of land to form an island, and the castle is situated on both sides of this chasm. Excavations carried out here and numerous finds of Mediterranean pottery have shown it was important in the fifth to seventh centuries, and in the thirteenth century Richard, Earl of Cornwall, the brother of King Henry III, built a huge castle here, probably because of its links with the by-then famous King Arthur.

"It's an enormous site," I say as we climb the steep path to the mainland courtyard. "We need to work out where Charlotte was when she drew her sketch, then we can try to find the crystal."

Arthur opens his mouth to speak, then glances over his shoulder. I stop and follow his gaze and say, "What?"

He frowns. "Nothing."

There are about a dozen people wandering around, a few couples and some families. I don't see anyone suspicious. But as my gaze skims across the scene, I get a similar prickling feeling that I did back at South Cadbury Castle. Someone's watching us. Someone who means us harm.

I swallow hard. "Come on. I'm sure she was on the island part of the castle."

Holding hands, Merlin at our side, we cross the footbridge to the island. The views are breath-taking, and we pause on the bridge and look across at the ocean, cold and forbidding even on a May afternoon. The wind is getting up, and the sky that was previously the colour of Arthur's eyes has turned iron-grey.

"He's here." Arthur's expression is stony. "He's brought the weather with him."

I notice that he's saying "he" and not "he or she" or "they". He's convinced it's Julian Bauer who's on our tail.

"Come on." I take his hand and lead him across the rest of the footbridge to the island.

There's so much to see here. We walk purposefully, but I can't help stopping to look at the remains of the castle, which must have looked amazing with the backdrop of the ocean. We walk through the garden that Earl Richard probably built in honour of the Arthurian love story of Tristan and Iseult. A stone monument reminds me that Iseult was the wife of King Mark—Arthur's king, Conomor.

"King Mark's wife had an affair with the knight, Tristan," I recall. "Did that really happen to Conomor? Is that why you have such a strong opinion on adultery and unfaithfulness?"

He nods. "It's one reason. The king was devoted to his wife. When he discovered she was having an affair, it nearly destroyed him. He was not an easy person to live with, but even so…" He looks pained, obviously remembering Conomor's suffering.

"It would have been difficult for women, though, wouldn't it?" I say. "Daughters were often used for political gain, and their feelings wouldn't have been taken into consideration. If a woman's husband was cruel or unloving, it would have been impossible to leave him. And if a man came along who showed her love and kindness, can she really be blamed for taking that opportunity? Don't we all deserve to be happy?"

"Happiness is a modern concept," he says, somewhat flatly. "Duty and honour are also important. Marriage vows are sacred and binding. We all have our roles to play."

He looks away, ending the conversation. That irritates me a little, but I remind myself he's a sixth-century man in a twenty-first-century body, and although he's made some amazing adjustments since he came out of the suit of armour, he's still going to have some hangovers from his previous life.

Deciding not to push it now, I let it go. We walk through the thirteenth-century castle and then down to the early medieval portion of the site. Low walls here mark houses that would have been standing during Arthur's time. He lets my hand fall, and I stand at the edge and watch him walk slowly across the grass, Merlin at his side. I can't blame him for being melancholy and out of sorts. It must be a strange feeling seeing the world you once knew now ancient and decayed.

Not wanting to disturb his thoughts, I get out Charlotte's sketch book and open it up. We're not in the right place. I can see these ruins in her sketch, but they're far off. She's not facing the cliffs, either. In the distance is a square building that looks castle-like; I'd assumed it was part of Tintagel, but it's too far away to be on the island. I turn in a circle, trying to find it on the horizon, and then I see it. Of course! It's the Camelot Castle Hotel. I haven't stayed there but I know it opened in 1899.

I turn 180 degrees and look across the windswept grass toward the cliffs. That's where Charlotte was standing.

"I think I've discovered where Charlotte was," I say to Arthur as he heads back to me. I point across the grass.

"Let's go," he says. "Too many memories here."

"I'm sorry." I slip my hand into his as we walk away, Merlin trotting in front. "I didn't realize how much of an effect this would have on you."

"It's not your fault. Most of the memories are happy. It just reminds me how much time has passed. It makes me feel out of place, like I don't belong."

I tighten my fingers around his. "Don't say that. Of course you belong here."

He stops walking then and turns me to face him. "Are you sure?" He speaks fiercely, but I'm shocked to see tears in his eyes. "I never realized it would take this long to come back," he whispers. He cups my face in his hands. "Morgana was supposed to find a way to heal my wounds and then return my spirit to my body. It was supposed to take days or weeks or maybe months. Not years. Not lifetimes."

And it's only then that I fully understand. Morgana only created a soulstone as a temporary device while she tried to heal Arthur's body. He was supposed to come back to me—to Guinevere—a short time later, still in the sixth century. But it didn't work. His wounds must have been too extensive, and he died anyway. So why didn't Morgana release his soul from the ruby when she realized she couldn't return him? Maybe the ruby was stolen, or perhaps they couldn't bear for him to be gone forever. Whatever happened, Arthur was in limbo, frozen in time until the moment I finally set him free.

Chapter Eighteen

I feel chilled to the bone. I assume it's Arthur's tale that's sent me cold, but when I look around I realize a mist has rolled in from the sea. It's like thick cobwebs, clinging to my clothes and hair, strong with the smell of seaweed.

"This is not a natural fog," Arthur says.

"Bauer?" I whisper. "Is he here?"

"I'm sure he is." His hand finds mine, and his other hand goes down to touch Merlin's head. "Whatever he has planned, he doesn't want people to see him do it."

"We need to get to the crystal," I tell him. "Come on."

I move in the direction of where Charlotte did her sketch, pulling Arthur with me. It's slightly uphill, the ground uneven with clumps of grass and buried stone, signs of a sleeping civilization. Our feet move slowly with the characteristic drag they seem to get when in the presence of a Calling Stone.

Despite my fear, I'm still in awe of the place. Arthur and I came to Tintagel in the sixth century; we visited the king here. It was important to us. I can almost feel the presence of those who have passed around us, watching us.

Out of the mist, a figure looms. I catch my breath—but it's just a statue. I've read about it before. It's called Gallos, an eight-foot-high bronze sculpture inspired by the legend of King Arthur and the history of Tintagel. It would have looked ghostly anyway, as it's only partially rendered, meaning that the rugged landscape is visible through gaps in the bronze, but it looks even more ethereal now, in the mist.

It stands almost on the edge of the cliff, on wet rock. The view out to the sea is obscured. I have the odd feeling of suspension, as if we're walking on cloud.

I can almost hear my pounding heart. Was this where Charlotte kissed Julian Bauer? Where she fell?

"This is it," I say, somewhat breathlessly as we near. "This is where Charlotte was standing when she drew the sketch."

"You think she buried the crystal here?" Arthur stops. His skin looks grey in the mist.

"I'm certain of it. Stay here."

Arthur bends forward, his hands on his knees, breathing heavily. I walk up to the sculpture, which towers above me, stretch out a hand, and place it on the cold bronze. The bearded figure wears a hooded cloak and rests his hands on the pommel of a sword that's point-down in the ground before him. It bears a striking resemblance to the Arthur I've seen in my visions, dancing with me at South Cadbury. Maybe the creator had a vision of his own?

I bend and place my hands on the rocky ground. It's icy cold. My breath frosts before my face. May in England can be cold, but I've never seen it frosty before.

The trouble is that there's nowhere to bury the crystal. I feel along the ground anyway, looking for any loose stones or holes, brushing away any earth. I find nothing, nothing... and then my fingers close over a small cold object in the middle of a clump of spiky grass. I lift it up—it's a wedding band.

I turn to Arthur. "It must be Charlotte's," I whisper. "I saw her take it off and drop it."

I stare at the gold ring and place it on my palm. Even though the ground must be cold and the air is frosty, the ring feels warm. I close my fingers around it.

I think of the Death card in the Tarot. Death is never final. It's only one step in the long journey from birth to rebirth. It's like being on a boat on a river. You can get off at any time...

The air around me shimmers. At first, I think it's the frost in the air, but then I blink and the mist clears. I'm still standing with Gallos behind me, but the day is blustery and sunny. And in front of me are Charlotte and Julian Bauer.

I'm peering through the veil of time. I shiver, even though I can feel the warm sun on my face.

Charlotte turns and looks straight at me, and my heart leaps as she walks toward me. But her gaze slides past, and I realize she's looking at the sculpture of Gallos. She passes me and goes right up to the statue. She takes something out of the pocket of her jacket and holds it up. The sun glints off its surface—it's a piece of rose quartz.

Out of her pocket, she retrieves another item—a tube of glue. Bauer comes forward to watch as she squeezes a blob of glue onto the crystal. She reaches behind the pommel of the sculpture's sword and presses the crystal there, holding it for a moment to make sure the glue has set before removing her hand.

She turns to Bauer, her eyes triumphant. "It's done," she says.

Bauer slides his hands into the pockets of his trousers. He's wearing the same navy suit as in my original vision, the same crisp white shirt and light-blue tie. I have no doubt that this is the same day.

He's good-looking, and as he gives Charlotte a sexy smile, I can completely see why she fell for him. He must have blown her away when he started paying her attention.

"He's ours?" he asks her.

She nods. "Now we've placed the final Calling Stone, we'll be able to lock onto him, wherever he is."

"You've done well," he replies. "We're a few days ahead. The king wants it done on the night of the new moon."

Wait, what? Who's the king?

And the night of the new moon? The various phases of the moon give different kinds of energy to spells. This king, whoever he is, obviously knows that. The new moon is a time for ending things, and I would imagine it's the perfect time for any kind of death ritual.

The new moon is today. Oh dear.

"When do I get to meet him?" Charlotte asks.

"Arthur?"

"No," she says. "The king."

"Soon," Bauer soothes. "Now, I think it's time for your reward." He gives her a sultry smile and pulls her into his arms.

She laughs and raises her arms around his neck as he lowers his lips to hers. I watch as she slips off her wedding ring and tosses it to the ground. My heart is heavy. I know what's going to happen, but I'm just a shadow here, powerless to stop anything.

Bauer lifts his head, and I have to watch Charlotte's happy expression turn to fear as she looks into his eyes. A heartbeat later, he shoves her hard, and she falls backward, over the edge of the cliff. I have one final glimpse of her terrified face before she vanishes.

Her expression is going to remain with me for a long, long time.

I blink, and the blustery, bright day vanishes. Thick mist descends, and Charlotte and Julian are gone. Arthur stands before me, his face filled with concern.

"I had a vision," I tell him. "I know where the crystal is."

I turn to Gallos and run my fingers over the pommel of the sword. I can feel the crystal, stuck to the rear of the pommel. I pick at the glue holding it there to try to remove it.

"I wouldn't do that if I were you."

We both whip around at the new voice. For a moment, I can't see where it's coming from. The mist has thickened, and it clings to us and the statue like a white blanket. Then the threads separate like cotton wool pulled apart, and I see a man standing before us. He's medium height, with cropped light-brown hair and a neatly trimmed beard. He's wearing a grey suit rather than the navy-blue business suit he wore in my vision, but there's no mistaking that it's Julian Bauer.

My heart pounds its fists on my ribs, but I don't move. I glance down as Merlin barks, half expecting him to leap at Bauer's throat, but Bauer holds out a hand, and the Labradoodle whimpers and backs away. Now I'm really afraid. That's powerful magic.

Bauer looks at Arthur. His expression is strange, full of curiosity and something else. As he moves closer, I realize it's hatred.

"So you're Arthur," he murmurs.

"I don't believe I've had the pleasure," Arthur replies.

Bauer walks forward until he's standing a few feet away from us. "You're not as tall as I thought you'd be," he says.

Arthur doesn't reply this time. He doesn't look afraid. He studies Bauer with interest. I wonder whether he's going to tell the other man that he has no idea what he's talking about, but instead he says, "Why have you been looking for me?"

"I have instructions to kill you."

I'm chilled to the bone. The thought of someone wanting Arthur dead is terrifying enough. But his words 'I have instructions' suggest it's not Julian's idea. I think of his words to Charlotte, *The king wants it done by Saturday at the latest.* As I feared, this goes much further and deeper than one guy with a grudge against Arthur.

"Do you have to kill me in any particular way?" Arthur asks.

"He left that up to me," Bauer replies.

"Who's he?" Arthur says.

Bauer just smiles and lifts a hand.

I run forward and stand in front of Arthur. "Don't," I say.

"Gwen!" Arthur grabs my arm and tries to pull me away, but I fight him. Bauer watches us with amusement.

"Guinevere," he states. "You were always going to come back to her, weren't you?"

"You don't want her, you want me." Arthur gives me a hard shove, and I stumble back, catch my heel on a rocky piece of ground, and fall onto my bottom. It hurts, but I ignore the stinging skin and scramble to my feet.

"You killed Charlotte Small," I snap.

"I did." He doesn't look the least bit surprised or repentant.

"Once she told you what you wanted, you dropped her like something you scraped off your shoe." My voice is bitter, even though I don't think I would have liked Charlotte, judging by what I've heard about her.

"Yeah," he says. "So what?"

My hands clench into fists. Against my hip, my phone vibrates, announcing that someone is calling me, but I ignore it, and after half a dozen rings, it stops.

"You're the worst kind of man," I say in a low voice. "Selfish, violent, and with no honour at all."

His eyes are blue, like Arthur's, but unlike Arthur's, which are the colour of a summer sky, Bauer's are a very light blue, almost white. They narrow now as he stares at me, and his smile fades.

"I saw you," I continue, frightened, but pleased his attention is on me and not Arthur.

Arthur reaches out and takes my hand. I wait for him to push me again, and he does, but in an odd way, a small nudge, away from him. He wants me to move.

I take a small, slow step to my left, away from the statue and Arthur, and Bauer turns to follow me.

"What do you mean?" he asks impatiently.

"I saw you here with Charlotte. She thought you were going to propose."

He sniggers.

"I saw the coldness in your eyes," I continue, the picture clear in my mind. "She knew what you were going to do."

"Good," he says, his voice sour. "She was a wet blanket. A waste of time."

"No," I say, "she wasn't." I'm still holding Charlotte's wedding ring, and I show it to him. It lies flat and cold on my palm.

He stares at it.

I pass it from my right hand to my left, then close my fingers around it. I hold it up to my mouth. Blow on it. And open my hand. The ring has vanished.

Bauer frowns. "What the—"

Arthur moves before he can finish. I have no idea why he asked me to distract Bauer, but out of the corner of my eye I see him step to the side, up to the towering figure of Gallos. Arthur wraps his hand around the hilt of the figure's bronze sword.

Thousands of visitors must have done the same over the years since it was brought here by helicopter. And of course the sword is fixed in place, welded to the rest of the statue.

But Arthur slides it easily out of the figure's grasp. Before Bauer can react, he lifts it in both hands and turns to face us.

I inhale sharply and step back. Merlin gets to his feet, and even as Bauer raises his hand and summons a ball of green light, I watch the Grail appear in front of us—a well of energy that glows brightly in the mist.

Arthur thrusts the sword point down into the centre of it. The Grail sends out a pulse—I feel it in every bone in my body, from my heels all the way up to my skull. As Bauer tosses the swirling green light toward us, Arthur moves the sword up. The green light meets the pommel and shatters the crystal.

Dangerous shards fly out. Bauer squeals and falls back, and Arthur and I both duck instinctively, covering our faces. The last thing I see is Merlin, standing between us, shards mystifyingly bending around him, his eyes reflecting the brilliant crystal light.

I blink and scrub my eyes, feeling as if I've looked into the flash of a camera. Slowly, my vision clears. The Grail has vanished. Merlin is still standing there, and he shakes himself, his woolly coat flying around him.

Arthur is moving across the rocky ground. Even as I walk forward, I see him knock Bauer back, and then he's on top of him, the sword pressed across his throat. Bauer's face is covered in nicks from the pieces of crystal, droplets of blood running down his cheeks and neck.

"Get up," Arthur yells, and he pushes himself to his feet and drags Bauer to his, keeping the point of the sword at his neck.

"Tell me who your master is," Arthur whispers, his voice filled with menace, "and I won't kill you."

I stand to one side, my heart racing. I have no doubt at that moment that he could and would thrust the sword into the man.

Bauer shakes his head. "I can't."

"You can, and you will." Arthur's voice brooks no denial. I can easily believe he commanded an army.

Bauer's eyes are full of fear. But suddenly I realize it's not Arthur he's afraid of.

"If I do, he'll kill me," he whispers.

"If you don't, *I'll* slit your throat," Arthur snarls.

Clearly, though, the threat of death at the hands of his master scares Bauer more. He wrenches himself away from Arthur's grip and stumbles back. Arthur curses and moves forward to grab him. But he's too late.

Julian Bauer pauses, then turns and steps over the cliff.

"No!" Arthur lunges for him, but Bauer has gone. The waves crash against the rocks, and then, as if someone's pulling aside a curtain, the mist clears, and the May sunshine covers the landscape like thick butter.

My hands come up to cover my mouth. Arthur stares after him for a long moment. Then he turns and comes over to me. He puts his arms around me, and I bury my face in his chest.

Chapter Nineteen

It feels as if we stand there for hours, but it can only be minutes before we hear footsteps coming up the pathway to the sculpture. Arthur glances over, and then he turns away. Keeping one arm around me, he slips the sword into the hands of the silent statue. It clips in neatly. When I reach out and put a hand on the pommel, it's solid, as if it's never been moved.

I turn to look at the source of the footsteps, and somehow I'm not shocked to see two police officers looking rather red-faced and out of breath, running toward us.

"Have you seen a man with light-brown hair and a beard, dressed in a grey suit?" one of them asks us.

I sigh and lean my head on Arthur's shoulder as he tells them what happened.

"We'll get a team looking for him," the officer says. "If you could stay here, please. My DCI wants to talk to you."

I look behind us. I'm not surprised to see Imogen coming up the steps.

She stops in front of us, and her sharp gaze searches my face.

"I'm all right," I tell her.

She takes my hand and pulls me to one side. "He threw himself off?" she asks.

I nod. "The last crystal was in the sculpture's sword. Somehow it exploded, and then Arthur managed to stop him casting a spell…" I'm still not sure what he did with the sword. How did he know to take it, and what actually happened?

"The official line is that Bauer came here," Imogen tells me firmly, "to the place where he killed his lover, wracked with remorse, and took his own life before you could stop him. Okay?"

"Okay. Immi, why did you come here today?"

"Matthew Hopkins rang me last night. He'd done some investigating of his own and discovered from Bauer's secretary that he'd disappeared for several hours the day Charlotte died. The secretary then admitted she'd seen a picture of Tintagel's website on his laptop before he left. Hopkins got in touch with the site and two members of staff confirmed they'd seen the two of them on that morning."

So Matthew did help. I still don't like the man, but I'm glad he did what he said he was going to do and investigated Bauer.

"Then," Imogen continues, "early this morning, Charlotte's body washed up about a mile or so along the coast. The two things were enough for me to be able to bring him in for questioning. I've had an unmarked car on him for a few days, so when the officers rang in to say it looked as if he was going to Tintagel, and then I got your text, I was worried he was following you."

"You called me back," I say, remembering that my phone rang.

She shakes her head. "I didn't want to worry you."

"Oh." I retrieve Charlotte's wedding ring from my pocket and offer it to Imogen. "I found this here. It's Charlotte's. She thought Bauer was going to propose to her."

She takes it and studies it. "How sad. Still, at least he's gone now. You're safe, right?" I hesitate, and she frowns. "What?"

"Bauer said to Arthur, 'I have instructions to kill you.' There's someone else, Immi. Someone behind all this. A man. Bauer called him the king."

"Elvis?" she asks.

I'm too much in shock to laugh. "He was terrified of him."

She doesn't say anything for a long moment. Then her phone rings, so she turns away and answers it. After a quick call, she comes back and says, somewhat cheerfully, "Well, one battle at a time, as I'm sure your boyfriend would tell you. The tide's out, so they've found Bauer's body on the rocks. You two can make a statement when you get back to Glastonbury."

"I'd like to see his ring, if he's wearing it," I tell her. "Hopkins said it had an unusual symbol on it, and we think it might mean he belonged to a coven."

"I'll check it out," she promises.

"If it's okay," Arthur says, joining us, "while we're here, I'd like to see Merlin's Cave."

"That's fine," Imogen replies. "Bauer's body is on the other side of the island."

"Thanks, Immi," I say.

"Look after her," she says to Arthur. "She's a bit pale."

"I will." He smiles at her and then leads me down the path, away from the statue in the direction of the early medieval settlement.

"Why do you want to go to Merlin's Cave?" I ask him as we navigate the path, Merlin at our side. I know it's a sea cave, only accessible at low tide.

"I'll show you when we get there." He holds my hand tightly. "Are you feeling okay?"

"I'm fine. Don't listen to Immi."

"You're probably in shock," he says as I shiver. "It was a horrific thing to witness." He puts his arm around me. I don't complain.

It's good that Bauer's gone, but the circumstances of his death and his suggestion that it's not all over yet are worrying.

But Imogen's right; one battle at a time. "Imogen called you my boyfriend," I mumble as we head down the path to the beach.

Arthur chuckles. "Makes me sound like I'm sixteen."

"I'm not sure what to call you. Friend, I suppose."

"Oh, I think we're more than friends, Gwen."

I look out, across the windswept waves. Ireland is over there somewhere. It's a beautiful day now the mist has gone, but I feel like the waves, all churned up and emotional. Will things change between us now the Calling Stones are destroyed?

"What happened up there?" I ask him. "With the sword, I mean. How did you know to pick it up?"

He takes my hand again. "That's the odd part. When you distracted Bauer with the ring, I heard singing."

"Singing?"

"You know that hymn you told me about?"

"You mean 'When a Knight Won His Spurs?'"

"Yes. I heard a female voice singing it. It was the last verse, the bit about the sword setting free the power of the truth. And suddenly I understood. The legend of Excalibur isn't about an actual sword. What it's saying is that faith and truth and honour are the weapons we need to wield against darkness."

I struggle to understand. "You're implying Excalibur is a metaphor. But then why were you able to take the sword from Gallos?"

"I don't know. But when I did, I felt…" He stops to navigate a steep part of the path and holds my hand so I don't slip.

"How did you feel?" I prompt as we continue down.

"Righteous," he says. "That sounds pretentious, but it's true. I'm not a saint. I have my faults—many of them, I'm sure. But I know right from wrong. I did back in the sixth century, when the Saxons tried to take our land, and I know it now."

He stops and looks out, shading his eyes against the afternoon sun. He's so handsome, it makes my heart ache.

"My warrior band might not have been the chivalrous knights from medieval legend," he says. "But they were good men. We didn't rape and pillage. We protected the king's people and looked after our land. We were honest and loyal. I think somehow the sword channelled that good energy and gave us more power from the Grail. I don't know how. I'm not an expert at these things."

I look down at Merlin, remembering the moment when the crystal exploded, and Merlin's eyes reflecting the light. I'm sure he knows more than he's letting on.

"Who do you think was singing?" I ask Arthur.

"No idea," he replies. "Maybe the Lady of the Lake?" He smiles. I smile back. One legend says the sword was returned to her, so maybe it's not as crazy as it sounds.

We've reached the bottom of the path. Arthur leads me through a pile of rocks and then across a sandy beach. I came here as a child, I think; I half remember it.

"Was this here in the sixth century?" I ask.

He nods. "We used to come here."

Oh, so maybe I remember it from when I was Guinevere. That gives me a strange tingle down my spine.

We walk along the water's edge, and I try not to think about Julian Bauer's broken body lying on the rocks on the other side of the island, or Charlotte, left floating in the sea for days until she finally washed up down the coast. I concentrate on watching Merlin's feet leaving footprints on the soft, wet sand, as Arthur leads us both into the cave.

It goes back a lot further than I thought, deep into the island. The first part of the floor is sand, the latter part turns rocky. I take out my phone to use it as a torch, only then remembering the phone call I received while we were talking to Bauer. Someone's left a message.

"Give me a sec." I go back to the entrance of the cave and dial my answerphone service. To my surprise, it's a message from Duncan Lyttle, who works at the field unit.

Half expecting him to advise me on working hours for next week, I'm surprised to hear his voice holding excitement as he says, "Gwen, we've heard from the coroner. He's had your coin hoard valued, and apparently there are some really rare coins in there. The British Museum immediately put in a bid for £430,000. That'll be split between John Farlow, who owns the land, and you. You'll get £215,000! I hope you're pleased with that! Ring us when you can. Bye."

I end the call and stand there for a minute. £215,000? It's such a vast amount of money to me that my brain can't compute.

I'm rich?

Correction—Arthur's rich. It's his money. I know he's going to insist that I have at least some of it, but I don't know if I can take it from him.

My heart racing, I switch the phone to torch mode and head back into the cave.

Arthur's deep inside, standing on a rock, lifting something down from a small hole high in the wall. As I watch, he slides a rock into the space that's obviously been shaped to fit it, because it completely hides the hole from view. He knew it was there; that's why he wanted to come here.

He steps down and walks toward me. I open my mouth to tell him about the phone call, but even as I go to speak, he holds out his hand.

An object rests on the centre. It's a ring. A simple gold band, inlaid with red stones.

Garnets.

He brushes his thumb across the surface and smiles at me.

"Is that…" I can't bring myself to say it.

He nods and hands it to me. "When we first came here, we discovered the hidey hole, and we used to leave little things for each other—messages and gifts. When I was wounded, you told me you'd hide the ring here and wouldn't wear it again until Morgana found a way to heal me. I only remembered when we were at South Cadbury Castle."

I turn the ring, watching the light from my phone illuminate the garnets. "This was my wedding ring?"

"All the way from India." He takes it from my palm, then lifts my hand to his mouth and touches his lips in the centre.

"Gwen," he says, "I can't imagine how difficult it's been for you. I turn up, practically on your doorstep, out of the blue, and you could have laughed in my face or walked off in the other direction, but you believed me. And you've waited for me."

"Not as long as you've waited for me," I remind him, my voice husky.

"Maybe. But it's more than any man can ask for. More than I deserve. What Charlotte did with the Calling Stones definitely had an effect on me. I felt distracted all the time, reluctant to talk about our lives together. But now..."

He looks at the ring for a long moment. Then, to my shock, he drops to one knee.

"Gwen Young," he says. "Will you make me the happiest man in the world and marry me? Again?"

Tears rush into my eyes. "Oh Goddess."

"Is that a yes?"

Merlin barks, and I laugh. "Oh yes, yes, yes!" I bend and fling my arms around his shoulders, and he laughs, gets back up to his feet, and swings me around.

Then he kisses me, a long, steamy, passionate kiss, making me tingle all over. I can barely breathe, let alone think, but suddenly it springs into my head.

"Oh, I nearly forgot!"

He laughs. "What?"

"That was Duncan on the phone. He's heard from the coroner. They've valued your urn of coins and you'll be getting £215,000. I'm sorry it's only half of the money, but half of it has to go to the landowner."

"I don't care." He kisses me again. "I'm thrilled to think I can pay you back a little for everything you've done for me."

I let him kiss me, my mind whirling. "You really want to marry me?"

"Of course I want to marry you. You're mine, Gwen. I want to be by your side for the rest of my life. I want to try to have children with you."

That really makes me sob. "Stop," I mumble, "I don't think I can take anymore."

He wraps his arms around me and kisses me again. "I love you," he murmurs against my lips. "So much."

"I love you too." And I kiss him back, as the waves crash on the rocks outside, and the May sun turns the surface of the ocean to diamonds.

Chapter Twenty

"At last," Imogen says, lifting her glass of champagne. "Something to celebrate!"

I laugh and clink my glass against hers, and we both take a sip of the sparkling liquid.

It's a week later, and we're at the Avalon Café, having an impromptu party to celebrate my engagement to Arthur. A lot of our friends are here: Beatrix and Max, Imogen and Christian, Delia and her husband, Brian, Melissa and her husband, Terry, Cooper, the young barista, and his new girlfriend, Tamara, Allison and Joss, who work in the café, Duncan, Una, and Kit from the field unit, Francis from the museum, the crew from the library and the Arthurian Adventure, and quite a few others. It's early evening, and people are spilling out onto the pavement with their drinks and nibbles to chat and listen to the live band—friends of Christian, who are playing folk music that makes me want to dance.

"To *double* celebrate," Christian corrects.

I lift my eyebrows. "What do you mean?"

His gaze slides to Imogen. "You haven't told her?"

"I didn't want to steal anyone's thunder," Imogen says, blushing.

"You've got to tell me now," I urge.

She looks up at Christian, a warmth in her eyes that the sassy, confident DCI normally keeps hidden. "Christian asked me to marry him."

I squeal and throw my arms around her, slopping champagne over the rim of my glass, and she laughs and hugs me back.

"That's wonderful news," Arthur says, shaking hands with Christian.

"It's so exciting," I tell Imogen. "Both of us getting hitched! Who'd have thought it?"

"Certainly not me," she admits. "I never thought I'd find a guy mad enough to put up with me."

"It's a chore," Christian says. "But someone's got to do it."

She grins and kisses him, and he nuzzles her neck and makes her laugh. Then she slides her arm through mine. "Are you sure you don't mind?"

"Why would I?" I ask, puzzled. "I'm thrilled for you."

Imogen looks at Arthur, and they exchange a smile. "Gwen doesn't do negative emotions," he reminds her.

"You're a darling," she says, and kisses my cheek.

"I've just had the best idea," I tell her. "Why don't we have a double wedding?"

She stares at me. "Are you serious?"

"Of course." Then I remind myself she might prefer to have the day to herself. "Well, it's just an idea. Obviously, you'd probably rather have two celebrations!"

"Oh, Gwen, no, I think it's a wonderful idea! Christian, what do you think?"

"I think it would be great," he says. "Moral support for each other on the day, eh, Arthur?"

"Definitely," Arthur says. "It'll be fun."

"Have you had any thoughts on where you want to get married?" Imogen asks me.

"I'd love to do it somewhere historical."

"Glastonbury Lake Village?" Christian suggests. "You could bring your wellies."

"I was hoping for something a little more upmarket," I say wryly.

"I love the idea," Imogen replies immediately. "A medieval castle. Or a stately home."

Christian says, "What about Wessex Castle?"

It's where Kit's going to start excavating next week. "Oh…" My jaw drops. Not only is it a glorious place, but it obviously also has a long history. "That would be perfect."

"I'll talk to Kit about it," Christian says. "See if he has any contacts at the castle."

"We could just go for it and rent Buckingham Palace," Arthur says.

Imogen sticks her tongue out at him, slides her arm through mine, and steers me away from the two laughing guys. "Pay no attention to them," she tells me. "We'll work out what we want and they can fall into line."

"Arthur won't mind, whatever it is," I say, smiling. "The only issue is that he doesn't want to wait very long!"

She glances over her shoulder at him, then puts her mouth closer to my ear. "Is he still being a gentleman, then?"

"He wants to wait until our wedding night," I reply. "Damn him."

She giggles, then hiccups, and puts her hand over her mouth. "Champagne bubbles."

I laugh, and we wander outside, into the balmy evening.

"By the way," she says, as we stop on the edge of the pavement looking out across Glastonbury Abbey, and sip our champagne. "I don't want to bring the mood down, but I've got something for you." She takes a piece of paper out of her pocket, opens it, and passes it to me.

It's a photo of a ring with a symbol in the middle—a triquetra in a circle, topped with two antlers. "Bauer's ring?" I ask.

She nods. "I'll email you the photo later. I thought it might be handy in tracking down any other members of Bauer's group. Do you have any idea who his boss might have been?"

I shake my head. "It must have been someone powerful, though, for Bauer to have been so afraid of him." I sip my drink. "What did you do with Charlotte's wedding ring?"

"Gave it back to her family. She had a brother. He didn't seem too upset over her death."

"Poor Charlotte," I say. "It seems as if very few people were sad to see her go."

"She doesn't deserve your pity." Imogen's voice is sharp. "She was helping Bauer to hunt Arthur down." She looks across, into the café, at where he's talking to Christian and Max. "How is he doing?"

"Better," I admit. "He's been a lot more open since we destroyed the Calling Stones. He's talked more about our lives back then, and how he feels about being here." I study the stones of the abbey, looking at how they glow in the late evening sun. "It was a mistake, you know."

"What was?"

"Him being in the suit of armour all that time. He thought Morgana was only putting his soul in the ruby until she could find a way to heal his wounds. He didn't realize he'd be there for nearly fifteen hundred years."

Imogen is silent for a moment. "Does he know what went wrong?"

"No. Obviously Guinevere went into a nunnery, so she must have known he wasn't coming back in her lifetime. What we don't know is whether she assumed his soul had passed on. I can't imagine that she knew he would be imprisoned in the ruby."

"Do you think Morgana did it on purpose?"

I shrug. "No idea."

I think then of the Tarot reading I did for myself a few days ago. I asked the Tarot for guidance and drew three cards. The first was the High Priestess. The second was the Emperor. The third was the Tower. All major arcana cards—all suggesting major influences at work. The Tower is a card of destruction and chaos—a stone tower struck by lightning, with figures tumbling from the top toward the ground. The Emperor sits on his throne in a position of power and authority. The High Priestess holds a book of magic and a crystal ball.

Is the Emperor Julian Bauer's boss, whoever he is? The High Priestess Morgana? And the Tower a sign of what's to come?

But I'm no expert at the Tarot, and the cards have many meanings. Although my initial instinct was to be afraid, I felt better when Arthur came in and drew the Four of Wands—a man and a woman dancing, which denotes weddings and celebrations. I'm getting married, and deep down I know it means more than just wearing Arthur's ring. I'm a modern woman, and I meant it when I said to him that I don't need saving. But there's a connection between us that's no ordinary bond. The passing of time has led to our love deepening and maturing, like whisky in an oak barrel. I'm his, and he's mine, and together I know we can face anything that Fate puts in our way.

Still, it's strange how I've drawn all those tens over the past few days. I still don't know what it meant. Maybe it was just coincidence. What else could it relate to?

Unbidden, Imogen's earlier words come into my mind when she talked about investigating Julian Bauer. *I've had a couple of officers start investigating him... He's a busy man. He travels to Number Ten a lot.*

Number Ten Downing Street? Is that what the cards were trying to tell me?

Is the 'king', whoever he is, also a politician? It would make sense, as the Emperor suggests he has power and authority. I wonder if any other politicians wear the same ring that Julian did?

"Earth to Gwen," Imogen says, telling me that I've zoned out again. "I'm in the mood for dancing, come on."

I don't want to think about it now. We've beaten the bad guy, and it's time to celebrate.

The two of us put down our glasses and start dancing to the music. We're soon joined by Arthur and Christian, and the four of us dance and laugh and dance some more as the sun slowly sets and floods the abbey with a beautiful red-gold light.

Her Wedding Knight (The Avalon Café Book 4)

Tonight's the knight...

At last, it's kitchen witch Gwen Young's wedding day to the gorgeous Arthur. They're having a double wedding with their best friends at Wessex Castle, a beautiful stately home. Everything goes swimmingly, until they discover that the castle is built on top of an Anglo-Saxon ship burial, and its owner bears an ancient grudge against them both…

Now available on Amazon!

*

Join the Avalon Café Readers!

Want to know when the next Avalon Café story is available? Join my mailing list to stay informed, and you'll also be able to download a free, exclusive short story (not for sale) about how Gwen met Merlin! Go to my website for more details:

Website: http://www.hermionemoon.com

About the Author

Hermione Moon writes cozy witch mysteries with a sprinkling of romance, set in Glastonbury, England. She also writes steamy contemporary romance as Serenity Woods, and is a USA Today bestselling author under that name. She currently lives with her husband in New Zealand.

Website: http://www.hermionemoon.com

Facebook: https://www.facebook.com/hermionemoonauthor